SECOND-CHANCE
SEDUCTION

KATE CARLISLE

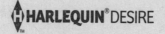

If you purchased this book without a cover you should be aware that this book is stolen property. It was reported as "unsold and destroyed" to the publisher, and neither the author nor the publisher has received any payment for this "stripped book."

Recycling programs
for this product may
not exist in your area.

ISBN-13: 978-0-373-73286-9

SECOND-CHANCE SEDUCTION

Copyright © 2013 by Kathleen Beaver

All rights reserved. Except for use in any review, the reproduction or utilization of this work in whole or in part in any form by any electronic, mechanical or other means, now known or hereafter invented, including xerography, photocopying and recording, or in any information storage or retrieval system, is forbidden without the written permission of the publisher, Harlequin Enterprises Limited, 225 Duncan Mill Road, Don Mills, Ontario M3B 3K9, Canada.

This is a work of fiction. Names, characters, places and incidents are either the product of the author's imagination or are used fictitiously, and any resemblance to actual persons, living or dead, business establishments, events or locales is entirely coincidental.

This edition published by arrangement with Harlequin Books S.A.

For questions and comments about the quality of this book, please contact us at CustomerService@Harlequin.com.

® and TM are trademarks of Harlequin Enterprises Limited or its corporate affiliates. Trademarks indicated with ® are registered in the United States Patent and Trademark Office, the Canadian Trade Marks Office and in other countries.

Printed in U.S.A.

www.Harlequin.com

Books by Kate Carlisle

Harlequin Desire

How to Seduce a Billionaire #2104
An Innocent in Paradise #2129
She's Having the Boss's Baby #2227
*Second-Chance Seduction #2273

Silhouette Desire

The Millionaire Meets His Match #2023
Sweet Surrender, Baby Surprise #2058

*MacLaren's Pride

Other titles by this author available in ebook format.

KATE CARLISLE

New York Times bestselling author Kate Carlisle was born and raised by the beach in Southern California. After more than twenty years in television production, Kate turned to writing the types of mysteries and romance novels she always loved to read. She still lives by the beach in Southern California with her husband, and when they're not taking long walks in the sand or cooking or reading or painting or taking bookbinding classes or trying to learn a new language, they're traveling the world, visiting family and friends in the strangest places. Kate loves to hear from readers. Visit her website, www.katecarlisle.com.

One

"You need a woman."

Connor MacLaren stopped reading the business agreement he was working on and glanced up. His older brother Ian stood blocking his office doorway.

"What'd you say?" Connor asked. He couldn't have heard him correctly.

"A woman," Ian repeated slowly. "You need one."

"Well, sure," Connor said agreeably. "Who doesn't? But—"

"And you're going to have to buy a new suit, maybe two," his brother Jake said as he strolled into his office.

Ian followed Jake across the wide space and they took the two visitors' chairs facing Connor.

Connor's gaze shifted from one brother to the other. "What are you two? The social police?"

Ian shook his head in disgust. "We just got off the phone with Jonas Wellstone's son, Paul. We set up a meeting with us and the old man during the festival."

Connor frowned at the two of them. "And for this you expect me to buy a new suit? You've got to be kidding."

"We're not kidding," Ian said, then stood as if that was the end of the discussion.

"Wait a minute," Connor insisted. "Let's get serious. The festival is all about beer. Drinking beer, making beer, beer-battered everything. This is not a ballet recital we're going to."

"That's not the point," Ian began.

"You're right," Connor persisted. "The point is that I've never worn a suit and tie to a beer festival and I'm not about to start now. Hell, nobody would even recognize me in a suit."

That much was true. Connor was far more identifiable in his signature look of faded jeans, ancient fisherman's sweater and rugged hiking boots than in one of those five-thousand-dollar power suits his two brothers were inclined to wear on a daily basis.

Frankly, this was why he preferred to work at MacLaren Brewery, located in the rugged back hills of Marin County, thirty miles north and a million virtual light years away from MacLaren Corporation in the heart of San Francisco's financial district. The brothers had grown up running wild through those hills. That's where they had built their first home brewery, in the barn behind their mom's house.

Over the past ten years, the company had grown into a multinational corporation with offices in ten countries. But the heart and soul of MacLaren Brewery still thrived in those hills, and Connor was in charge of it all: not just the brewery, but also the surrounding farmland, the dairy, the fishery, the vineyards and the brew pub in town.

And he wasn't about to wear a freaking business suit while he did it.

Meanwhile his older brothers, Jake, the CEO, and Ian, the marketing guru, took care of wheeling and dealing at their corporate headquarters in San Francisco. They both lived in the city and loved the fast pace. Connor, on the other hand, avoided the frantic pace of the city whenever possible. He only ventured into headquarters on days like this one because his brothers demanded his presence at the company's board meetings once a month. Even then, he wore his standard outfit of jeans, work shirt and boots. He'd be damned if he'd put on a monkey suit just to discuss stock options and expansion deals with his brothers.

Connor glanced at the two men, who were closer to him than any two people on the planet. "What made you think I would ever dress up for the Autumn Brew Festival? I'd be laughed off the convention floor."

True, the festival had become a very important venue for the fast-growing, multibillion-dollar beer production industry. In the past few years it had expanded to become the largest gathering of its type in the world. The powers that be had even changed the name of the event to reflect its importance. It was now called the International Brewery Convention, but Connor and his brothers still called it the festival because more than anything else, people showed up to have a good time.

It was a point of pride that the festival was held annually in their hometown at the Point Cairn Convention Center next to the picturesque marina and harbor. It was one of the biggest draws of the year, and the MacLaren men had done their best to ensure that it continued to be a not-to-be-missed event on the calendars of beer makers and breweries around the world.

But that still didn't mean Connor would dress up for it. What part of "good time" did his brothers not understand? The words did not equate with "suit and tie" in anybody's dictionary.

Jake gazed at him with a look of infinite patience. As the oldest of the three, he had perfected the look. "Wellstone's scheduled a dinner meeting with all of us and his entire family. And the old man likes his people to dress for dinner."

"Oh, come on," Connor said, nudging his chair back from the desk. "We're buying out their company. They're dying to get their hands on our money so the old man can retire to his walnut farm and enjoy his last days in peace and quiet, surrounded by nuts. Why would he care one way or another how we dress for dinner?"

"Because he just does," Jake explained helpfully. "His son, Paul, warned us that if Jonas doesn't get a warm and cozy, old-fashioned family feeling from the three of us at dinner, there's a good chance he could back out of the deal."

"That's a dumb way to do business."

"I agree," Jake said. "But if it means snagging this deal, I'll wear a freaking pink tuxedo."

Connor frowned. "Do you honestly think Jonas would back out of the deal over something so minor?"

Ian leaned forward and lowered his voice. "It happened to Terry Schmidt."

"Schmidt tried to buy Wellstone?" Connor peered at Jake. "Why didn't we know that?"

"Because Wellstone insists on complete confidentiality among his people," Jake said.

"I can appreciate that."

"And Paul wants it to stay that way," Jake continued, "so keep that news under your hat. He only brought up the Schmidt situation because he doesn't want another deal to fail. He wants our offer to go through, but it all depends on us putting on a good show for Jonas. Apparently the old man's a stickler."

Ian added, "Terry blew the deal by wearing khakis and a sweater to dinner with the old man."

"Khakis?" Shocked, Connor fell back in his chair. "Why, that sociopath. No wonder they kicked him to the curb."

Ian snickered, but just as quickly turned sober. "Jonas Wellstone is definitely old school. He's very conservative and very anxious that the people who take over his company have the same family values that he has always stood for."

"He should've gone into the milk shake business," Connor muttered.

"Yeah, maybe," Jake said. "But look, he's not about to

change, so let's play the game his way and get the old man firmly on our side. I want this deal to go through."

Connor's eyes narrowed in reflection. "Believe me, I want that, too." Wellstone Corporation was a perfect fit for MacLaren, he mused. Jonas Wellstone had started his brewery fifty years ago, decades before the MacLarens came along. He had been at the front of the line when lucrative markets in Asia and Micronesia first began to open up. Yes, the MacLarens had done incredibly well for themselves, but they had to admit they were still playing catch-up to the older, more established companies. Last year, the brothers had set a goal of acquiring a strong foothold in those emerging territories. And here they were, less than a year later, being presented with the opportunity to purchase Wellstone.

So if all it took to attain their objective were some spiffy new clothes, the decision was an easy one. Connor would go shopping this afternoon.

"Okay, you guys win." He held up his hands in mock surrender. "I'll buy a damn suit."

"I'll go with you," Jake said, adjusting the cuffs on his tailor-made shirt. "I don't trust your taste."

The hand gesture Connor flipped his brother was crude but to the point. "This is the reason I hate coming into the big city. I get nothing but grief from you two wheeler-dealers."

Ian stood to leave. "Spare us the country bumpkin act. You're more of a cutthroat than we are."

Connor laughed and stretched his legs out. "My rustic charm conceals my rapier-sharp business skills."

Ian snorted. "Good one."

Jake ignored them both as he checked his wristwatch. "I'll have Lucinda clear my schedule for this afternoon."

"Fine," Connor said. "Let's get this over with."

Jake nodded. "I'll swing by here around three and we'll

head over to Union Square. We've only got a week to buy you a suit and get it tailored. You'll need shoes, too. And a couple of dress shirts."

"Cuff links, too," Ian added. "And a new belt. And a haircut. You look like one of Angus Campbell's goats."

"Get outta here," Connor said, fed up with the whole conversation. But as his brothers headed for the door, Connor suddenly remembered something. "Wait. What was that you said about needing a woman?"

Ian turned back around but didn't make eye contact. "You need to bring a date to dinner. Jonas likes to see his partners in happy relationships."

"And you didn't tell him that's a deal breaker?"

Ian scowled and walked out as Jake and Connor exchanged glances.

"Just find a date," Jake said finally. "And don't piss her off."

Definitely a deal breaker, Connor thought.

Abandon hope, all ye who enter here.

There should've been a sign announcing that sentiment, Maggie Jameson thought as she stared at the massive double doors that led to the offices of MacLaren International Corporation. But Maggie wasn't about to give up hope. She was on a mission, so rather than whimper and crawl away, she summoned every last bit of courage she could muster and pushed through the doors to announce herself to the pleasant, well-dressed receptionist named Susan at the front desk.

"He's expecting you, Ms. James," Susan said with a genuine smile. "Please follow me."

James? You had to give them a fake name to even get near him, the voice inside her head said, jeering. *Walk away before they toss you out on your ear.*

"Shush," Maggie whispered to herself.

But the sarcastic little voice in her head wouldn't stay silent as Maggie followed the charming receptionist down the wide, plushly carpeted halls. And as if to amplify the mental taunts, everywhere she looked there were signs that the MacLaren brothers had succeeded beyond anyone's wildest dreams. Huge posters of the latest MacLaren products hung on the corridor walls as she passed. Lush plants grew in profusion. Glassed-in office spaces boasted state-of-the-art furnishings and technology.

Maggie was even treated to the occasional stunning view, through wide windows, of the gleaming San Francisco Bay in the distance. Just in case she forgot that this was the penthouse suite of the office building owned by the MacLaren Brothers of Point Cairn, California. As if she could.

Despite her best efforts, Maggie felt a tingle of pleasure that Connor MacLaren had done so well for himself.

Yeah, maybe he'll give you a nice, shiny medal for doing him such a big favor.

Maggie sighed and glanced around. The receptionist was many yards ahead of her down the hall, and Maggie had to double her speed to keep up. How long was this darn hallway anyway? Where was Connor's office? In the next county? She should've left a trail of bread crumbs. If she had to leave in a hurry, she'd never find her way out. Heck, she could wander these corridors for years. It was starting to feel as if she was stuck on some kind of never-ending death march.

Stop whining. Just turn around and walk away before it's too late.

If she had a choice, she would take her own subliminal advice and hightail it out of there. She'd taken a big risk coming here and now she was regretting it with every step she took. Hadn't she spent half of her life avoiding risks? So why in the world was she here?

Because she didn't have a choice. She was desperate. Truly, completely desperate. Connor MacLaren was her last hope.

But he hates you, and for good reason. Walk away. Walk away.

"Oh, shut up!"

Susan stopped and turned. "Is something wrong, Ms. James?"

Yes, something's wrong! That's not my real name! Maggie wanted to shout, but instead she flashed a bright smile. "No, absolutely nothing."

As soon as the woman continued walking, Maggie rolled her eyes. Not only was she talking to herself, but now she was arguing with herself, too. Out loud. This couldn't be a good sign.

Her life truly had descended to the lowest rung of the pits of hell, not to be overly dramatic about it.

Even the cheery receptionist had caught on to the desperation vibe that hung on Maggie like a bad suit. She had taken one look at Maggie's faded blue jeans and ancient suede jacket, and smiled at her with so much sympathy in her eyes that Maggie wouldn't be surprised to have the woman slip her a ten-dollar bill on her way out.

Treat yourself to a hot meal, sweetie, Maggie imagined the woman whispering kindly.

Unquestionably, Maggie had been hiding out in the remote hills of Marin for way too long. Glancing down at her serviceable old jacket and jeans, she realized that she'd lost the ability to dress for success. Her boots were ancient. She hadn't been to a beauty spa in more than three years. True, she hadn't exactly turned into a cave dweller, but she certainly wasn't on top of her fashion game, either. And while that wasn't a bad thing as far as Maggie was concerned, it was probably a mistake not to have factored it in when she was about to go face-to-face with one of Northern California's top power brokers.

The man whose heart everyone believed she'd broken ten years ago.

Someday she would find out why Connor had allowed everyone in town to believe it was her fault they'd broken up all those years ago. It wasn't true, of course. They'd had what could charitably be called a mutual parting of the ways. She could remember their last conversation as if had happened yesterday because Maggie was the one who'd ended up with a broken heart. Her life had changed drastically after that, and not in a good way.

Why had her old friends turned their backs on her and blamed her for hurting Connor so badly? Had he lied about it after she left town? It didn't seem like something Connor would have done, but she had been away such a long time. Maybe he had changed.

Maggie shook her head. She would never understand men and she wasn't even sure she wanted to. But someday she would ask him why he did it. Not today, though, when she had so many bigger problems to deal with. She didn't dare take the risk.

Turn around. Walk away.

"Here we are," Susan the receptionist said cheerfully as she came to a stop in front of another set of intimidating double doors. "Please go right in, Ms. James. He's expecting you."

No, he isn't! He's not expecting a liar!

Maggie smiled stiffly. "Thank you, Susan."

The woman walked away and Maggie faced the closed doors. She could feel her heart pounding against her ribs. The urge to walk—no, *run*—away was visceral. But she'd come this far on sheer nerves, so there was no way she would walk away now. Besides, even if she did try to leave, she'd never find her way out of this office maze.

"Just get it over with," she muttered, and praying for strength, she pushed on the door. It opened silently, gliding across the thick carpeting.

At her first glimpse of Connor, Maggie's throat tightened. She tried to swallow, but it was no use. She would just have to live with this tender, emotional lump in her throat forever.

He sat with complete ease behind an enormous cherry wood desk, unaware that he was being watched as he read over some sort of document.

She was glad now that she'd made the appointment to see him here in his San Francisco office instead of facing him down back home. Not only would she avoid the gossip that would've invariably erupted when people found out she'd been spotted at the MacLaren Brewery, but she also would've missed seeing him backlit by the gorgeous skyline of San Francisco. Somehow he fit in here as well as he did back home.

For a long moment, she simply reveled at the sight of him. He had always been the most handsome boy she'd ever known, so how was it possible that he was even more gorgeous now than she remembered? He was a man now, tall, with wide shoulders and long legs. His dark, wavy hair was an inch or two longer than was currently fashionable, especially for a power broker like him. She had always loved his remarkable dark blue eyes, his strong jawline, his dazzling smile. His face was lightly tanned from working outside, and his well-shaped hands and long fingers were magical…

A wave of longing swept through her at the thought of Connor's hands and what he was capable of doing with them.

Maggie sighed inwardly. Lovemaking was one aspect of their relationship that had always been perfect. Yes, Connor had taken too many foolish risks with his extreme sports, and yes, Maggie's fears for his safety had driven her crazy sometimes and had ultimately led to their breakup. But when it came to romance, theirs had been a match made in heaven.

Maggie remembered her grandpa Angus saying that the MacLaren brothers had done well for themselves. Now, observing Connor in this luxury penthouse office, she could see that Grandpa's comment had been a gross understatement. She probably had no right to feel this much pride in the brothers' accomplishments, but she felt it anyway.

At the thought of her grandfather, Maggie dragged her wandering mind back to the task at hand. Grandpa Angus was the main reason she was daring to show her face here today.

Connor hadn't noticed her yet, and for one more fleeting moment, she thought about turning and running away. He would never have to know she had been here and she would never have to experience the look of anger and maybe pain in his eyes. And he would never know to what extent she'd been willing to risk humiliating herself. But it was too late for all that. She had been running from her mistakes ever since she first left Connor, and it was time to stop.

"Hello, Connor," she said at long last, hoping he couldn't hear the nerves jangling in her voice.

He looked up and stared at her for a long moment. Had she changed so much that he didn't even recognize her? But then one of his eyebrows quirked up, and not in a "happy to see you" kind of way.

He pushed his chair away from the desk and folded his arms across his muscular chest. After another lengthy, highly charged moment, during which he never broke eye contact with her, he finally drawled, "Hello, Mary Margaret."

The sound of his deep voice made the hairs on her arms stand at attention. Amazingly, he still retained a hint of a

Scottish accent, even though he'd lived in Northern California since he was in grade school.

Anxious, but determined not to show it, she took a few steps forward. "How are you?" Her voice cracked again and she wanted to sink into the carpet, but she powered forward with a determined smile.

"I'm busy." He made a show of checking his watch, then stood. "I'm about to go into a meeting, so I'm afraid I don't have time to talk right now. But thanks for stopping by, Maggie."

She deserved that, deserved to have him blow her off, but it hurt anyway. She took slow, even breaths in an effort to maintain her dignity, for she had no intention of leaving. "Your meeting is with me, Connor."

He smiled patiently, as though she were a recalcitrant five-year-old. "No, it's not. Believe me, I would never have agreed to meet with you."

She said nothing as she watched him study her for several long seconds until she saw the moment when realization struck.

"Ah, I get it," he said evenly. "So you're Taylor James. Inventive name."

"Thank you," Maggie murmured, even though she could tell by his tone that he wasn't the least bit impressed by her cleverness. She'd managed to use part of her real last name and had come up with a first name that could be male or female. She tugged her jacket closer. Had the temperature dropped in here? Probably not, but she felt a chill right down to her bones.

"Why the subterfuge, Maggie?"

She kept her tone as casual as she could manage. "I wanted to see if I could make it in the business without leaning on my family name." It was the same lie she'd been telling herself for the past three years she'd been back in Point Cairn. The truth was too embarrassing to admit.

"How intrepid of you," he said dryly.

She watched for a smile or even a scowl, but Connor revealed nothing but indifference. No real emotion at all. She had anticipated something more from him. Hurt. Anger. Rage, even. She could've accepted that. But Connor didn't appear to be fazed one way or the other by anything she said or did.

That's where the chill came from. She shivered again.

But honestly, what did she expect? Happy hugs? Not likely since she'd found out that he'd considered her departure such a betrayal. But if his current mood was any indication, he had obviously moved on long ago.

And so did you, she reminded herself.

He circled his desk and leaned his hip against the smooth wood edge. "I heard you've been back in town for a while now. Funny how we've never run into each other."

"I keep a low profile," she said, smiling briefly. The fact was, she'd spotted him a number of times on the streets of their small hometown of Point Cairn. Each time, she'd taken off running in the opposite direction. It was self-protection, plain and simple, as well as her usual risk aversion.

She'd returned to Point Cairn three years ago in a low state, her heart and her self-confidence battered and bruised. There was no way she would've been strong enough to confront Connor on his home turf. Not back then. She was barely able to do so right this minute. In fact, she could feel her thin facade beginning to crack and wondered how much longer she could be in his presence without melting down.

"How's your grandfather?" he asked, changing the subject. "I haven't seen him in a few weeks."

She smiled appreciatively. He and his brothers had always had a soft spot for Angus Campbell, and the feeling was mutual. "Grandpa is…well, he's part of the reason I've come to see you today."

He straightened. "What's wrong? Is he ill?"

Maggie hesitated. "Well, let's just say he's not getting any younger."

Connor chuckled. "He'll outlive us all."

"I hope so."

He folded his arms again, as if to erect an extra barrier between them. "What is it you want, Maggie?"

She reached into her bag and pulled out a thick folder. "I want to discuss your offer."

He reached for the folder, opened it and riffled through the stack of papers. They were all letters and copies of emails sent to someone named Taylor James. Many had been signed by Connor, himself, but there were offers from others in there, too. He looked at Maggie. "These were sent to Taylor James."

"And that's me."

"But I was unaware of that fact when I made those offers. If I'd known Taylor James was you, Maggie, I never would've tried to make contact." He closed the folder and handed it back to her. "My offer is rescinded."

"No." She took a hasty step backward, as though the folder were on fire. "You can't do that."

For the first time, his smile reached his eyes. In fact, they fairly twinkled with perverse glee as he took a step closer. "Yes, I can. I just did."

"No, Connor. No. I need you to—"

In a heartbeat, his gaze turned to frost. "I'm not interested in what you need, Maggie. It's too late for that."

"But—"

"Meeting's over. It's time for you to go."

For the briefest second, her shoulders slumped. But just as quickly, she reminded herself that she was stronger now and giving up was not an option. She used her old trick of mentally counting from one to five as she made one last effort to draw from that sturdy well of self-confidence she'd fought so hard to reconstruct.

Defiantly she lifted her chin and stared him in the eyes. "I'm not leaving this office until you hear what I have to say."

Two

He had to admire her persistence.

Still, there was no way Connor would play this game with her. At this point in his life, he wanted less than nothing to do with Mary Margaret Jameson. Yes, they'd been high school sweethearts and college lovers. At age twenty-two, he'd been crazy in love with her and had planned to live with her for the rest of his life. But then she'd left him with barely a word of warning, moved to the East Coast and married some rich guy, shattering Connor's foolish heart into a zillion pieces. That was ten years ago. At the time, he vowed never to be made a fool of again by any woman, especially Maggie Jameson.

Except it now looked as if she'd succeeded in fooling him again. All it took was a convenient lie. But then, he'd found out long ago just how good Maggie was at lying.

The last time they'd spoken to each other was on the phone. How screwed up was it that Connor could still remember their final conversation? He'd been about to go on some camping thing with his brothers and she'd mentioned that she wouldn't be there when he got home. How could he have known she meant that she *really* wouldn't be there? Like, gone. Out of his life. Forever.

Well, until today. Now here she was, claiming to be the very person he'd been trying to track down for months.

Odd how this mystery had played itself out, Connor thought. Eighteen months ago, a fledgling beer maker began to appear on the scene and was soon sweeping medals and gold ribbons at every beer competition in the western states. The extraordinary young brewmeister's name was Taylor James, but that was all anyone knew about "him." He never showed up in person to present his latest formulation or to claim his prize, sending a representative instead.

Taylor James's reputation gained ground as the quality of his formulas grew. He won more and more major prize categories while attracting more and more attention within the industry.

And yet no one had ever seen him.

Connor had been determined to find Taylor James and, with any luck, buy him out. Or hire him. But he hadn't been able to locate him. Who was this person making these great new beers and ales while continuing to hide himself away from his adoring public? For the past year, Taylor James had continued to beat out every other rival. Including, for the first time ever, MacLaren's Pride, the pale ale that had put the MacLaren brothers on the map and helped them make their first million. Losing that contest had been a slap in the face and had made the MacLarens even more determined to find the mysterious beer maker.

Through one of the competitions, Connor was able to obtain Taylor James's email address and immediately started writing the guy. He received no answer. From another competition, Connor unearthed a post office box number. He began sending letters, asking if the elusive brewer would be interested in meeting to discuss an investment opportunity. He never heard a word back—until this moment.

Now as he stared at the woman claiming to be the reclusive new genius of beer making, Connor was tempted to toss the fraudulent Ms. James out on her ear. It would be even more fun to call security and have her ignominiously escorted out to the sidewalk. The shameful exit might give her a minuscule taste of the pain and humiliation he'd endured when she walked out of his life all those years ago.

But that would send the wrong signal, Connor reasoned. Maggie would take it as a sign that he actually cared one way or the other about her. And he didn't. The purely physical reaction to her presence meant nothing. He was a guy, after all. And he had to admit he was curious as to why she'd hidden herself away and worked under an assumed name. She was a talented brewer, damn it. Her latest series of beers and ales were spectacular. And why wouldn't they be? She came from a long line of clever Scottish brewers, including her grandfather Angus, who had retired from the business years ago.

So he'd give her a few minutes to tell her story. And then he'd kick her excellent behind right out of his office.

With a generous sweep of his hand, he offered her one of the visitors' chairs. Once she was seated, he sat and faced her. "You've got five minutes to say whatever you came to tell me, Maggie."

"Fine." She sat and cleared her throat, then smoothed her jacket down a few times. She seemed nervous, but Connor knew better. She was playing the delicate angel, a role she had always performed to perfection.

He scowled, remembering that he used to call her his Red-Haired Angel. She still had gorgeous thick red hair that tumbled down her back, and her skin was still that perfect peaches and cream he'd always loved to touch. God, she was as beautiful as she was the day he met her. But she was no angel. Connor had learned that the hard way.

"My formulas have won every eligible competition for the past eighteen months," she began slowly, picking up speed and confidence as she spoke. "I've singlehandedly transformed the pale ale category overnight. That's a quote from the leading reviewer in the industry, by the way. And it's well deserved. I'm the best new beer maker to come along in years."

"I know all that." Connor sat back in his chair. "It's one of the reasons why I've been trying to hunt down Taylor James all these months. For some reason, *he* didn't feel compelled to respond."

"*He* wasn't ready," she murmured, staring at her hands.

Connor was certain that those were the first truthful words she'd uttered since walking into his office.

She pursed her lips as if weighing her next sentence, but all Connor could think was that those heaven-sent lips were still so desirable that one pout from her could twist his guts into knots.

His fists tightened. He was about to put an end to this nonsense when she finally continued to talk.

"Here's my offer," she said, leaning forward in her chair. "I'll sell you all of those prizewinning formulas and I'll also create something unique and new for MacLaren. It'll be perfect as a Christmas ale and you'll sell every last bottle, I guarantee it."

"At what price, Maggie?"

She hesitated, then named a figure that would keep a small country afloat for a year or two. The amount was so far out in left field, Connor began to laugh. "That's absurd. It's not worth it."

"Yes, it is," she insisted. "And you know it, Connor. You said it yourself. The Taylor James brand is golden. You'll be able to use the name on all your packaging and advertising and you'll make your money back a thousand times over."

She was right, but he wasn't going to admit that just yet. He stared at her for a minute, wondering what her real motivation was. Why had she come to him? There had to be other companies that wanted to do business with her. Or rather, with *Taylor James*.

"Why now, Maggie?" he asked quietly. "Why do you want to sell those formulas? And why sell to me?"

"Why?" She bit her luscious bottom lip and Connor had to fight back a groan. Irritated with himself as much as he was with her, he pushed himself out of his chair and scowled down at her. "Answer me, Maggie. Tell me the truth or get the hell out of here. I don't have time for this crap."

"You want the truth?" She jumped up from her chair and glared right back at him. "Fine. I need the money. Are you happy? Does it fill your heart with joy to hear me say it? I'm desperate. I've been turned down by every bank in town. I would go to other beer companies, but I don't have the time to sift through bids and counteroffers. I need money now. That's why I came to you. I've run out of choices. It's you or…"

She exhaled heavily and slid down onto the arm of the chair. It seemed that she'd run out of steam. "There. That's it. Are you happy now?"

"At least I'm hearing the truth for once."

She looked up and made a face at him. He almost laughed, but couldn't. She'd expended all her energy trying to finagle a deal with him and she just didn't have it in her. She might well be the worst negotiator he'd ever dealt with. And for some damn reason, he found it endearing.

For his own self-preservation, he'd have to get over that feeling fast.

"Where did all your money go?" he asked. "You must've gotten a hefty settlement from your rich husband." He gave her a slow up-and-down look, taking in her faded jeans and worn jacket. "It's obvious you didn't spend it all on shoes."

"Very funny," she muttered, and followed his gaze down to her ratty old boots. After a long moment, she looked up at him. "I know what you must think of me personally, but

I'm too close to the edge to care. I just need a loan. Can you help me or not?"

"What's the money for?" he asked.

She pressed her lips together in a stubborn line, then sighed. "I need to expand my business."

"If you're selling me all your formulas, you won't have a business left."

"I can always come up with new recipes. My Taylor James brand is going strong, growing more profitable every day. And my new Redhead line is popular, too."

"Then what's the money for?" he asked again, slowly, deliberately.

"I need to upgrade my equipment. I need to hire some help. I need to develop a sales force." She sighed and stared at her hands. "I need to make enough money to take care of my grandfather."

He frowned. "You mentioned Angus earlier. Is something wrong with him?"

It was as if all the air fled from her lungs. Her shoulders slumped and God help him, he thought he saw a glimmer of tears in her beautiful brown eyes.

"He's been to the hospital twice now. It's his heart. I'm so worried about him. He runs out of breath so easily these days, but he refuses to give up his goats. Or his scotch."

"Some things are sacred to a man."

"Goats and scotch." She rolled her eyes. "He insists that he's hale and hearty, but I know it's not true. I'm scared, Connor." She ran one hand through her hair, pushing it back from her face. "He needs medication. They have a new drug that would be perfect for someone in his condition, but we found out it's considered experimental. The insurance won't cover it and it's too expensive for me to pay for it."

Connor frowned. This wasn't good news. Angus Campbell was one of the sweetest old guys he'd ever known. Connor and his brothers were first inspired to make their own beer while watching Angus at work in the Campbell family pub. That brew pub had been on Main Street in Point Cairn for as long as Connor could remember. Growing up, he and his brothers had all worked there during the summer months.

Then five years ago, Angus lost his beloved wife, Doreen. That's when Maggie's mom sold the pub to the MacLaren brothers. Angus insisted that she move to Florida to live with her sister, something she'd been talking about for years. But that left Angus alone with his goat farm, though he got occasional help from the neighborhood boys. This had all happened during the time Maggie was living back east with her rich husband.

Now Maggie was back home and the only family she had left in Point Cairn was her grandpa Angus.

Connor made a decision. "I'll pay for that medication."

"We don't need charity, Connor."

Her words annoyed him at the same time as he admired her for saying them. "I'm not talking about charity, Maggie. Call it payback. Angus was always good to us."

"I know," she said softly. "But he's almost eighty years old. There'll be lots more medication in the future, along with a hundred other unexpected expenses. I need cash going forward to get my brewery up and running. That way, I'll be able to generate enough funds of my own to pay for Grandpa's health care needs." She started walking, pacing the confines of his office as if she couldn't bear to stand still any longer. "I'll also be able to hire some workers for both me and Grandpa and maybe make a few improvements to the farm. I'm looking to arrange a business deal, Connor. A fair trade, not a handout. And I need to do it right away."

"What happened at the bank?"

"I expected them to come through, but they turned me down. They explained that with the economy and all…" She gave a dispirited shrug.

Connor had been watching her carefully. He had a feeling there was something she wasn't telling him. Why wouldn't the bank loan her the money? Even though she was divorced, she must have received a hefty settlement. Her beers and ales were kicking ass all over the state, so she had to be considered a good risk. Was she hoarding the settlement money away for some reason?

And another thing. She and her grandfather owned at least a hundred acres of prime Marin farmland that would make excellent collateral for any bank loan.

She might not be lying to him at the moment, but she was holding back some information. Connor would pry it out of her eventually, but in the meantime, a plan had been forming in his mind as they talked. If he wasn't mistaken, and he rarely was, it would be the answer to all their problems. She would get her money and he would get something he wanted.

Call it restitution.

"I'll give you the money," he said.

She blinked. "You will?"

"Yeah." He hadn't realized until Maggie showed up today that he still harbored so many ambivalent feelings for her. Part of him wanted to kick her to the curb, while another more rowdy part of him wanted to shove everything off his desk and have his way with her right then and there.

He thought she had a lot of nerve showing up here asking for money. And yet he also thought she showed guts. It was driving him nuts just listening to her breathe, so why shouldn't he pull her chain a little? Just to settle the score.

"What's the catch?" she said warily.

He chuckled. Once again, she'd thrown him off base. She should've been doing cartwheels, knowing she'd get the money, but instead she continued to peer suspiciously at him.

"The catch," he explained, "is that it won't be a loan. I want something in return."

"Of course," she said, brightening. "I've already promised you the Taylor James formulas."

"Yeah, I'll take those formulas," he said, "but there's something else I want from you."

Her eyes wide, she took a small step backward. "I don't think so."

"Take it or leave it, Maggie," Connor snapped.

"Take or leave what?" she said in a huff. "I don't even know what you're talking about."

He shoved his hands in his pockets. "It seems I need a date."

"A date?" she scoffed. "You must know a hundred women who would—"

"Let me put it this way. I need a woman who knows a little something about beer. You more than meet that requirement, so I intend to use your services for a week."

"My...*services?* What are you talking about?"

"I'm talking about taking you up on your deal. I'll pay you the entire amount of money you asked for in exchange for your formulas, plus this one other condition."

"That I'm at your *service* for a week? This is ridiculous." Agitated, she began to pace the floor of his office even faster.

"It's only for a week," he said reasonably. "Seven days and nights."

"Nights?" she repeated, her eyes narrowing.

He shrugged lightly, knowing exactly what she was thinking. Sex. "That's entirely up to you."

"This is blackmail," she muttered.

"No, it's not. I'm about to give you a lot of money and I want something in return."

"My services," she said sarcastically.

"That's right. Look, the Autumn Brew Festival is next week."

"I know that," she grumbled.

"I need a date, and you're the perfect choice. So you will agree to be my date the entire week and go to all the competition events with me. I'll also want you to attend a number of meetings and social events with me, including the Friday night gala dinner dance."

That suspicious look was back. "Are you kidding?"

"What? You don't like to dance?"

She looked stricken by his words but quickly recovered. "No, I don't, as a matter of fact."

That was weird. Maggie had always loved dancing. "Doesn't matter," he said. "You're going to the gala."

"We'll see about that." Her eyes focused in on him. "And that's it? We pal around for a week at the festival and I get the money?"

"That's it. And I'll expect you to stay with me in my hotel suite."

She stopped and stared at him. "Oh, please."

"You want the money or not?"

"You know I do, but I can drive in and meet you each morning."

"That won't work. I expect us to keep late hours and I have a number of early morning breakfast meetings scheduled. I don't want to take any chances on you missing something important."

"But—"

"Look, Maggie. Let me make it clear so there's no misunderstanding. I don't expect you to sleep with me. I just expect you to stay at the hotel with me. It'll be more convenient."

She frowned. "But I can't leave Grandpa for that long a time."

"My mother will look in on him," he said, silently patting himself on the back for his split-second problem-solving abilities. Deidre MacLaren had known Angus for years, so Connor knew she wouldn't mind doing it.

"And at the end of the week," he continued calmly, "I'll give you the money you asked for in full."

"And all I have to do is stay with you for a week?"

"And be my date."

"In your hotel room."

"It's a suite."

"I'll sleep on the couch."

"You'll be more comfortable in a bed."

"And you'll sleep on the couch?"

"No."

Her eyes widened. "Stop kidding around."

His lips twitched. "Am I?"

"Wait," she said suddenly. "I'll get my own room."

"The hotel is sold out."

A line marred her forehead as she considered that for a moment, and then she brightened. "We can switch off between the couch and—"

"Take the deal or leave it, Maggie."

She flashed him a dark look. "Give me a minute to think."

"No problem."

She took to pacing the floor again, probably to work out the many creative ways she would say *no* to his outlandish offer. But she would definitely say no, wouldn't she?

Hell, what in the world was he thinking? God forbid she agreed to his conditions. What would he do in a hotel suite with Maggie for a week? Well, hell, he knew what he *wanted* to do with her. She was a beautiful woman and he still remembered every enticing inch of her body. He'd never forgotten all the ways he'd brought her pleasure. Those thoughts had plagued him for years, so living with her for a week would be a dangerous temptation. It would be for the best if she refused the offer.

And once she turned him down, Connor would go ahead and pay for Angus's medication, even if he had to sneak behind her back to do it. And as for Maggie getting a loan to grow her business, he figured that would happen eventually. She'd either find a bank that would agree to it or she'd tap one of the other brewery owners.

That thought didn't sit well with him, though. He didn't want anyone else getting their hands on her beer formulas. Or her, either, if he was being honest.

And in case he'd forgotten, he still needed a date for the Wellstone dinner meeting. As much as he hated to admit it, Maggie would be perfect as his date. Jonas Wellstone would fall in love with her.

So maybe he'd gone too far. If she turned him down— hell, *when* she turned him down, he would simply renegotiate to get those formulas and to convince her to be his date at the Wellstone dinner. That's all he really wanted.

Meanwhile, he had to chuckle as he watched her stomp and grumble to herself. A part of him wanted to take her in his arms and comfort her—in more ways than one. But once again, that wayward part of him was doomed to disappointment, because other than the obvious outward attraction to her, Maggie meant nothing to him now, thank goodness. He counted himself lucky that he'd gotten over her duplicity years ago. This offer of his was just sweet payback, pure and simple. It felt damn good to push some of her buttons the way she'd pushed his in the past, saying one thing but meaning something else. Keeping him in a constant state of confusion. Now it was his turn to shake her up a little.

"So what's your answer, Maggie?" he asked finally.

On the opposite side of the room, Maggie halted in her pacing and turned to face him. A big mistake. She could feel his magnetic pull from all the way over there. Why did he still have to be so gorgeous and tall and rugged after all these years? It wasn't fair. She could feel her hormones yipping and snapping and begging her to take him up on his offer to spend a week together in that hotel suite of his.

What was wrong with her? Unless she'd missed the clues, he was clearly out for revenge, pure and simple. Imagine him insisting that she provide him *services* for a week. Even though he'd assured her that she wasn't expected to sleep with him, she had a feeling he wasn't talking about a plain old dinner date here and there.

Services, indeed!

At that, her stomach nerves began to twitch and buzz with excitement. *Services!*

Oh, this wasn't good.

"Maggie?"

"Yes, damn it. Yes, I'll do it," she said, waving her hands in submission.

He hesitated, then took what looked like a fortifying breath. "Good."

"But I won't sleep with you." She pointed her finger at him for emphasis.

He tilted his head to study her. "I told you I don't expect you to."

"But…the hotel suite." She let go of the breath she didn't know she'd been holding. "Okay. But…never mind. Good. Fine. That's fine." She stopped talking as she felt heat rise up her neck and spread to her cheeks. She tended to turn bright pink when she was embarrassed, so Connor probably noticed it, too. Even though he'd made it clear he didn't want to sleep with her, she'd assumed…well. That's what she got for assuming anything. Apparently he just wanted to keep tabs on her.

If she'd thought about it for a second or two, she would've realized that he could have any woman he wanted. They

probably waited in line outside his door and threw themselves at him wherever he went. Why would he want to
sleep with Maggie, especially after he'd spent all these years
thinking she had betrayed him? All he wanted was a date,
someone who knew something about the brewery business.
And that description fit her perfectly.

"I misunderstood," she admitted.

"Yeah, you did," he said, his tone lowering seductively
as he approached her. "Because if you and I were to do
what your mind is imagining, Maggie, there wouldn't be
much sleeping going on."

Staggered, Maggie felt her mouth drop open. "Oh."

"So it's settled," he said, breezily changing tempo again
as he tugged her arm through his and walked her to the
door. "I'll pick you up Sunday morning and we'll drive together. Be sure to pack something special for the gala and
a few cocktail dresses. We'll be dining with a number of
important business associates, and I want them to walk
away impressed."

She refused to mention that she only owned two simple
cocktail dresses and nothing formal, having given away
most of her extensive wardrobe to the local consignment
shop three years ago. Instead she turned and jabbed her
finger in his chest for emphasis. "Just so we're clear, Connor. I'm not going to have sex with you."

He looked down at her finger, then up to meet her gaze.
"Still negotiating, huh?"

She whipped her hand away and immediately missed
the sizzle of heat she'd gotten from touching his chest. She
told herself it meant nothing. It had just been a while since
she'd touched a man. Like, years. No wonder she was getting a contact high.

"I'm serious, Connor," she said, hating that her voice
sounded so breathless. "I'll share your room with you, but
that's it."

"It's a suite," he corrected, and slowly leaned over and kissed her neck.

Dear Lord, what was he doing? She knew she should slap him, push him away, but instead she shivered at the exquisite feel of his lips on her skin.

"Say it with me," he murmured. "Suite."

"Suite," she murmured, arching into him when he gently nipped her earlobe. This had to stop. Any minute now.

"Sweet," he whispered, then pulled her into his arms and kissed her.

Three

The heat was instantaneous. Maggie felt as if she were on fire and she reveled in the warmth of his touch. She couldn't remember feeling this immediate need, not even years ago when she and Connor first made love. And certainly not in all her years with Alan Cosgrove, her less than affectionate ex-husband.

Good grief, why was she thinking about a cold fish like Alan when Connor's hot, sexy mouth was currently devouring her own?

She gripped his shirt, knowing she ought to put an end to this and leave right now. Talk about taking a risk! This was madness. She had to stop. But oh, please, no, not yet. For just another moment, she wanted to savor his lips against hers, his touch, his strength, his need. It had been much too long since any man had needed her like this.

Connor had always been a clever, considerate lover, but now he was masterful as he maneuvered her lips apart and slid his tongue inside to tangle with her own, further melting her resistance. His arms encircled her, his hands swept up and down her back with a clear sensual awareness of her body as his mouth continued to plunder hers.

And just at the point where she was ready to give him anything he wanted, Connor ended the kiss. She wobbled, completely off balance for a moment. She wanted to protest and whine for him to kiss her again. But she managed to control herself, taking time to adjust the shoulder strap of her bag and straighten her jacket.

Then she glanced up and caught his self-satisfied smile. He looked as if he'd just won a bet with someone, maybe himself.

She remembered that smile, remembered loving it, loving him. Times changed, though, and just because they'd shared an amazing kiss didn't mean she had any intention of sleeping with him. Still, at least she knew what she was up against now. Was she crazy to have such strong feelings for him after so many years? No, it would only be crazy if she acted on those feelings. She needed to remind herself of the only thing that mattered: getting the loan, by almost any means necessary. Which meant that she would walk through fire to get it. And Connor MacLaren was fire personified.

She took a deep breath and struggled to maintain a carefree tone. "I guess I'll see you Sunday, then."

"Yes, you will." And with a friendly stroke of her hair, Connor opened the office door. "Drive home safely."

"I will. Goodbye, Connor."

She strolled from his office in a passion-soaked haze. But despite her earlier concerns, she somehow found her way out of the large office maze and down to the parking garage. And before she knew it, she was driving toward the Golden Gate Bridge and heading for home.

The kiss meant nothing, Connor assured himself as he closed his office door. He'd just been trying to teach her a lesson. Testing her. Keeping her on her toes. He'd wanted to prove she was lying when she claimed she wouldn't dream of having sex with him. And, he told himself, he'd done a hell of a job. She had practically ripped his shirt off right there and then. Hell, if he hadn't put an end to the kiss when he did, they would be going at it naked on his office couch by now.

And didn't that paint a provocative picture? Damn. The

image of her writhing in naked splendor on the soft leather couch was stunning in its clarity, causing him to grow rock hard instantly. In his mind's eye, he could almost touch the gentle slope of her curvaceous breasts, could almost taste her silky skin.

"Idiot," he muttered, straining to adjust himself before settling back to work. "Explain again why you stopped kissing her?"

At the time, it had made sense to stop, he argued silently. But now, as he hungered for more…he shook his head. Maggie had always had the ability to tie him into knots and now she was doing it again. Damn it, he was a different man than he was ten years ago. Stronger. Smarter. He wasn't about to let her call the shots again. He would be the one in control of the situation while they were together next week.

But the voice inside his head began to laugh. *Control. Good luck with that.*

He ruthlessly stifled that mocking voice. So maybe he hadn't always had a firm grip on things when he was with Maggie before. Things were different now. He still didn't trust her as far as he could throw her, which was pretty far, seeing as how she'd lost some weight since he'd last seen her. She was just as beautiful, though. Maybe more so. When he first looked up and saw her standing in his office doorway, she had taken his breath away. She'd always had that power over him, but he was older and wiser now and not about to fall for her charms again.

He wouldn't mind kissing her again, though, and was momentarily distracted by the searing memory of his mouth on hers. And it went without saying that he would do whatever it took to get her into bed with him. He was a red-blooded man, after all. Didn't mean he cared about her or anything. It was just something he'd be willing to do if the occasion presented itself—and he had every intention of making sure that the occasion presented itself.

Absently, Connor checked the time. Damn, he only had twenty minutes before Jake would show up to drag his ass out to shop for a new suit. He figured he'd better get some real work done in the meantime so he'd be ready to go when Jake got here. His brother had already warned him that he'd be on the phone with the Scottish lawyers this afternoon, and that always put Jake in a foul mood.

The lawyers from Edinburgh had been trying to convince one of the MacLaren brothers to fly to Scotland to take care of the details of their uncle Hugh's estate. Whoever made the trip would be stuck there for weeks. But that wasn't the real reason none of them wanted to go there. No, it was because Uncle Hugh had been a hateful man. Jake, Ian and Connor couldn't care less about the terms of Hugh's last will and testament, despite the fact that they were his beneficiaries, in a manner of speaking.

Even though Connor and his brothers had grown up around Point Cairn in Northern California, they'd been born in the Highlands of Scotland. They were the sons of Liam MacLaren and heirs to Castle MacLaren. But when Connor was a baby, their uncle Hugh, an evil bastard if ever there was one, swindled their father out of his inheritance.

Their dad never recovered from the betrayal and died a few years later, leaving their mother, Deidre, a widow with three young boys to raise. Unwilling to live in the same area as her despised brother-in-law, she moved with her boys to Northern California to be near her sister. Connor had no memory of any other home except the rugged hills that overlooked the wild, rocky coast of Marin County.

Connor stared out the office window at the stunning view of the Golden Gate Bridge and the Marin shoreline beyond. Maybe in some small way, their uncle had done them all a favor because Connor couldn't imagine living anywhere else in the world. Hell, he never would have met Maggie Jameson otherwise, he thought, and then wondered if that was a good thing or a bad thing. He wasn't ready to decide on that one, but he couldn't help smiling in anticipation of spending the following week in a hotel suite with the gorgeous woman.

By the time she arrived home, Maggie felt relatively normal again. Her heart had finally stopped hammering in her chest, and her head had ceased its incessant buzzing. All that remained from Connor's onslaught was a mild tingling of her lips from his devastating kiss.

Mild? That was putting it, well, mildly. But never mind his kiss. What about his demands? For someone so risk-averse, Maggie still couldn't believe she'd entered the lion's den and put herself in such a perilous position. After all the lectures she'd given herself and all the positive affirmations she'd memorized, she had taken one look at Connor and practically rolled over, allowing him to take hold of the situation and make choices for her.

She pulled her car into the garage next to the barn and walked across the circular drive to the large ranch-style home she shared with her grandfather. The afternoon sun barely managed to hold its own against the autumn chill that had her tugging the collar of her old suede jacket closer to her neck. She still took a moment to appreciate the land that rolled and dipped its way down to the sheer bluffs that overlooked the rough waves of the Pacific Ocean. Despite some sorry choices in her past, she had to marvel at her own good luck. She was home now, living in a beautiful house in a magical location. Her darling grandfather, despite some tricky health issues, was still kicking, as he liked to put it. She was proud of herself, proud of how she'd finally arrived here, both emotionally and physically.

Connor MacLaren had no idea how much it had cost

her to show up at his office door with her hat in her hand, and Maggie had no intention of ever revealing that to him. She'd fought too hard to get to where she was today, and she wasn't about to gamble it all away on some *tingling* feeling she'd received from a simple kiss.

She jogged up the porch stairs and into the house, where she checked the time on the mantel clock. Her grandfather would be out in the barn milking his goats. Dropping her bag on the living room chair, she went to her bedroom to make a phone call. She was determined to avoid sharing a hotel room with Connor—even if it *was* a luxurious penthouse suite, as he had emphasized more than once.

But when she called the convention hotel to make a reservation, she was told that they were sold out, just as Connor had warned. And when she called the next closest hotel, she was quoted a price that was so far out of her range she almost laughed out loud at the reservationist.

She merely thanked her instead and hung up the phone. Then she spent a few minutes at her computer, searching for information. Finally, with nervous fingers, she dialed Connor's number.

"MacLaren," he answered.

"It's Maggie and I've been thinking, Connor," she began. "It's probably best if I commute to the festival from home after all. Grandpa isn't well and I'd rather be home each night to see him."

"I've already talked it over with my mother, Maggie," Connor replied dryly. "She plans to stop by your place twice a day and spend the night there, too. I know Angus won't put up with two women fussing at him day and night, so you'll be doing him a favor by staying away for the week."

"I'm not sure if—"

"And besides," he continued in steamroller fashion, "you've already agreed to be my date for the week, remember? In exchange for which I'm going to give you a lot of money. I think that's a pretty good deal for you."

"Pretty good deal," she echoed darkly.

"Maggie, I explained all this to you and I thought you had agreed. I'm going to need you to accompany me every day, starting with breakfast meetings and going into the late evenings with all the social events I've got to attend."

She frowned into the phone. "You never liked all that social stuff before."

"That was true ten years ago," he said smoothly. "Now I figure it's a small price to pay to get what I want."

"The price of doing business?"

"Exactly. And it won't hurt you to be seen with me, Maggie. It'll be good for your business to meet the people I know, too."

She knew he was right about that. But still. "Okay, but I'm not going to the dance."

"You're going with me, Maggie."

"You don't know what you're asking."

There was a moment of silence, and then Connor said, "Are you saying this is a deal breaker?"

Her shoulders slumped as she recognized that hard-nosed tone of his. She wasn't about to break their deal, but she still had no intention of attending the stupid dance. Especially because it wasn't just a dance. Maggie had looked it up on the festival website. The dinner dance was actually a formal affair, a gala event, meant to celebrate the culmination of the festival year and probably as snooty as any high-society ball she had ever attended in Boston. But since she didn't want to argue anymore, she left it alone for now. After a minute more of conversation, she disconnected the call.

She couldn't tell him that she didn't mind being his date for all the events during the week. That wouldn't be any problem at all. But the thought of having to share his hotel suite with him? It made her want to run through the house screaming. She didn't know how she would manage it, but unless another hotel room opened up in the next few days, she would soon find out.

But even another hotel room wouldn't fix the somewhat smaller dilemma of her not attending the dance. Maggie groaned and pushed that little problem away. If they managed to make it through the week together, Connor would just have to understand.

None of this would've been necessary if the banks hadn't turned down her loan. But the money was critical now. Even though Grandpa insisted that he was still hale and hearty and fit as a fiddle, Maggie was so afraid that one of these days he would need more care than she could afford to give him. She had gone through most of her meager settlement money fixing the roof of the house and then she'd bought a number of replacement items for the brewery.

She had been hoping to use the remaining funds as collateral, but now that Angus needed expensive medication and possibly even surgery someday, she'd reached the point of desperation. Her business was on the verge of expanding into a wider market, and that would bring in more money eventually, but before that happened, she needed to raise some capital to keep things going. And that was where Connor came into the picture. Negotiating and trading her beer formulas for cash was better than going to the bank. This way, she wouldn't have to pay back a loan.

She suddenly felt so tired and gazed at her comfortable bed longingly. How nice it would be to climb under the covers and take a long nap, but first she wanted to help Grandpa feed the goats.

As she stripped out of her "nice" jeans and pulled on her old faded pair, she had to laugh at herself. A few years ago, she wouldn't have dreamed of wearing jeans to a meeting in the city. Not even her "nice" jeans. But happily, jeans and work shirts had gradually replaced most of the clothing she'd worn during her marriage.

Alan, her ex-husband, had expected her to dress up every day, usually in smart skirts and twin sweater sets with pearls. It didn't matter what she was planning to do that day.

"You must always be seen wearing fashionable yet sensible clothing," her ex-mother-in-law, Sybil, was forever reminding her, usually in a scolding tone of voice.

Three years ago, when Maggie first arrived back in Point Cairn after her divorce, she'd had no idea what an emotional mess she was. She just knew that her marriage had gone disastrously wrong and she was determined to get past the whole experience and move forward. She wanted to catch up with old friends and explore the town she'd missed so dearly. So one day, shortly after she'd returned, she drove into Point Cairn to do the grocery shopping.

While at the store, she ran into some of her old high school friends she hadn't seen in years. She was thrilled to reconnect, but they quickly put her in her place, telling her they wanted nothing to do with her. They were still resentful that she had turned her back on the town. More important, they were livid that she'd hurt Connor so badly all those years before. Her friends had made it clear that while Connor was still universally loved and admired by one and all, Maggie was most assuredly *not*. One friend put it more succinctly: Maggie could go stuff it as far as they were concerned.

It was another blow to Maggie's already fragile self-esteem and she had limped home to cry in private. For a full month afterward, she lived in her pajamas, wandering in a daze from her bed to the couch to watch television and then back to bed again. The thought that she might've hurt Connor was devastating to her, but the notion that Connor had lied to her old friends about their mutual breakup was just as bad. Why would he do that?

She remembered tossing and turning at night, unable
to sleep for all the pain she might have caused—without
even meaning to do so!

Then one day, her grandfather told her he could really
use her help with the goats.

Maggie's spirits had lifted. Grandpa needed her! She had
a reason to get dressed and she did so carefully, choosing
one of her many pastel skirts and a pale pink twinset with
a tasteful gold necklace and her Etienne Aigner pumps.

When she walked into the barn, Grandpa took one look
at her and asked if she thought they were going to have a
tea party with the goats. He chuckled mightily at his little
joke, but Maggie jolted as if she'd been rudely awakened
from a bad dream. She stared down in dismay at her outfit,
then ran from the barn and stumbled back to the house in
tears. Poor Grandpa was bewildered by her behavior and
blamed himself for upsetting her.

But Maggie knew where to place the blame. It was her
own damn fault for being so weak, so blind and so stupid.
She'd been well programmed by her manipulative ex-husband and could still hear his sneering voice in her head,
telling her what to do, how to behave, what to wear and
what she'd done wrong. As soon as their wedding vows
were exchanged, Alan's disapproval began and never let
up. It had come as such a rude shock and she realized later
that she'd been in a terribly vulnerable state after leaving
Connor. Otherwise, she might have recognized the signs
of cruelty behind Alan's bland exterior.

During her marriage, she'd occasionally wondered why
she ever thought Connor's love of extreme sports was too
risky for her when compared to the verbal assaults she received constantly from her husband and his mother.

Maggie still couldn't get the sound of their menacing
intonations out of her head.

She had thought that by moving three thousand miles

away from her ex-husband and his interfering mother, she would be rid of their ruthless control over her. But the miles didn't matter. Alan and Sybil were still free to invade Maggie's peace of mind with their disparaging comments.

That moment in the barn with Grandpa provided Maggie with a sharp blast of reality that quickly led to her complete meltdown. For days, she couldn't stop crying. Grandpa finally insisted on taking her to the local health clinic to talk to a psychologist. But how could she make sense of something so nonsensical? All she knew was that everything inside her was broken.

Gradually, though, Maggie came to realize that she was not to blame for succumbing to Alan's masterful manipulations. Through the outpatient clinic, she met other women who'd survived similar relationships. And she discovered, quite simply, that if she stayed busy with chores and projects, she didn't have time to worry and fret about the past. Oddly enough, it was Grandpa's quirky flock of goats that helped her get through the worst of it.

Lydia and Vincent Van Goat, the mom and dad goats, didn't care what Maggie was wearing or whether she was depressed or flipping out. They just wanted food, and Lydia and the other girls needed to be milked. The milk had to be weighed and recorded, then taken to the local cheesemongers to be turned into goat cheese and yogurt. The goats demanded fresh water to drink and clean straw to sleep on. Their hooves needed trimming. The newest goat babies needed special care and eventually, weaning.

They couldn't do any of it by themselves; they needed Maggie to help them survive. Maggie soon realized that she was dependent on them for her survival, too. The goats gave her a reason to get out of bed every morning. She had priorities now, in the form of a flock of friendly, curious goats.

For the next six months, much of Maggie's energy was spent tending the goats. She filled out her days by preparing meals for Grandpa and taking long walks along the cliffs and down on the rough, sandy beach. She grew a bit healthier and happier every day.

Eventually she was able to acknowledge that Grandpa was perfectly able to do most of the work with the goats himself. Thanks to Grandpa, Maggie was nearly back to being her old self, which meant that it was time for her to find a real job and make some money. Sadly, the idea of working in town where she could run into her former friends was just too daunting. That's when Grandpa suggested that while she was figuring things out, she might enjoy dabbling in her father's old family beer-making business.

The microbrewery equipment lay dormant in the long, narrow storage room next to the barn. Her father had called the room his brew house, and it was where he used to test some of the beers they served at their brewpub in town. The storage room had been locked up for years, ever since her dad died.

Maggie had fond memories of following her father around while he experimented with flavors and formulas to make different types of beers, so the idea of reviving his brew house appealed to her. Within a week, she was hosing down and sanitizing the vats, replacing a few rusted spigots and cleaning and testing the old manual bottling and kegging equipment her father had used. She spent another few weeks driving all over the county to shop for the proper ingredients and tools before she finally started her first batch of beer. And it wasn't half bad.

That was three years ago. Now Maggie could smile as she tapped one of the kegs to judge the results of her latest pale ale experiment. She had entered this one in the festival and fully expected, or *hoped,* anyway, to win a medal next week.

Once her glass was filled, she made a note of the liquid's

light golden brown appearance, then checked its aroma. Next, she tasted it, trying to be objective as she tested its flavor and balance.

"Perfect," she murmured. It just might be her best formula yet. Finished for the day, she closed off the valve and cleaned up the counter area, then took her small glass of ale out to the wide veranda that circled the house. There she relaxed and finished her drink as she watched the sun sink below the cliffs.

At this time of the afternoon, it wasn't unusual to spot a family of black-tailed deer or the occasional tule elk foraging its way past live oak trees, arroyo willows and elderberry shrubs. Maggie spied a brush rabbit scurrying across the trail, seeking cover from a red-tailed hawk that glided in the sky.

Maggie loved the wild beauty of these hills, loved the scent of sea salt in the air. She never got tired of staring at the windblown, impossibly gnarled cypress trees that lined the bluffs at the edge of the property. When she was young, she'd been certain that elves lived in those trees. Everything was magical back then.

The magic seemed to disappear after her father died. His death had marked the beginning of too many bad choices on Maggie's part. In the past few years, though, she had managed to turn things around and was now determined to bring some of that old magic back. That was one reason why the revival of her father's beer-making legacy was so important to her.

The upcoming Autumn Brew Festival would be the culmination of all her struggles to establish herself as a key player in the industry her father had loved. Maggie had come a long way and was proud to be the owner and operator of "possibly the best new small brewery in Northern California," as one critic had called her burgeoning enterprise.

But her smile faded as she was reminded again of the deal she'd struck with the devil, aka Connor MacLaren. If Maggie's old high school friends had anything to say about it, Connor should feel entirely justified in seeking his revenge next week. The slightest negative word from Connor would be enough to destroy Maggie's standing among her industry peers.

If Maggie was being honest, though, she would have to admit that it wasn't Connor's style to be vindictive or mean. On the other hand, he had blamed her for the breakup and might be willing to do something to get even with her over the next week.

But while the possibility of dirty tricks and sabotage alarmed her, Maggie's real concern was Connor himself and his dangerous proximity. How was she expected to survive a full week in the same hotel suite with him? For goodness' sake, the man had only improved with age to become the sexiest creature she'd ever seen. Maggie knew full well that he had every intention of luring her into bed with him. Could she possibly resist his sensual onslaught? Did she even want to?

She left that question unanswered, but she was adamant that whatever occurred, it would be by her own decision. She would never again allow herself to be coerced by a man. She was no longer a weak-kneed, passive girl but a confident, successful woman in control of her own destiny. And she would decide if that destiny included a sexy roll in the hay with Connor MacLaren.

The strong, confident woman giggled at that image as she went inside to start dinner.

Later, as they dined on meat loaf, mashed potatoes and freshly harvested green beans, she and her grandfather talked about the festival. "I'm afraid I'll be gone all week, Grandpa."

"I'm glad you're getting out and having some fun," he

said jovially. "And don't you worry about me. I'll be fine while you're gone."

"I won't worry," Maggie said, "because Mrs. MacLaren has already promised to stop by for a visit every day."

"That wasn't necessary," Grandpa muttered, but Maggie could tell his grumbling was just for show. He and Deidre MacLaren, Connor's mother, were lifelong friends and would have a great time visiting. More important, Mrs. MacLaren was a retired nurse so she would be able to tell in an instant if anything was wrong with Grandpa.

Maggie thought the rest of the week would drag on forever, but almost before she knew it, Sunday morning arrived and so did Connor MacLaren. She met him outside as he pulled up to the house in a shiny black pickup truck. Ignoring the sudden rush of heat she felt as she watched him approach, she carried her overstuffed suitcase awkwardly down the porch steps. He met her halfway, took the bag and easily lifted it into the back of his truck.

"I hope you have room for my kegs," Maggie said.

"That's why I brought the truck," he said, and followed her to the beer house. They made several trips back and forth, carrying the heavy kegs and securing them in the truck bed.

"Just one more thing," Maggie said, running back to the beer house. She emerged a minute later with a dolly loaded with three cases of bottled beer for the official judging.

"I guess I don't have to ask if you've entered the competition yourself," he said dryly.

"I honestly wasn't sure I would until the last minute," she admitted. "But the festival is so important I had to give it a try. But don't worry, I'm only entered in the small brewery category so I won't be competing with MacLaren."

"Good," he muttered. "You beat our asses off last time."

"I did, didn't I?" She smiled broadly.

As he loaded the cases, he noticed the markings on the box tops. "You've entered under your real name?"

"Yes." She sighed. "I decided it was time to come out of the shadows."

"Good. People should know who they're dealing with."

Was he talking about himself being deceived by her false name? Maggie kept silent, figuring the less said about that, the better.

He opened the passenger door and held her arm as she climbed up into the cab. Maggie almost groaned as her arm warmed to his touch.

"Should be an interesting contest," Connor said lightly, and slammed her door shut.

Something about his tone aroused Maggie's suspicions and they grew as she watched him circle the truck and jump into the driver's seat.

"Let me guess," she said, her heart beginning to sink. "You're one of the judges."

It was his turn to smile as he slipped the key into the ignition and started up the truck. "Yeah. Problem?"

"Oh no," she said glumly. "What could possibly go wrong?"

"No need to worry, Maggie. It's a blind tasting."

"Then why are you wearing such an evil grin?"

As Connor chuckled, she settled in for the ride.

Four

As soon as they arrived at the convention center hotel, they stowed their belongings with the bellhop, who would hold everything until their room was ready. One of the festival handlers took her kegs and assured her that they would be delivered to the beer garden, where many of the brewers served their latest beers to the festival goers all week long. Maggie took personal custody of the dolly that held the three cases she'd designated for the competition. Then Maggie and Connor went their separate ways.

Maggie could finally breathe again. The tension in the truck had been palpable and she wondered for the umpteenth time how she would survive a week in a hotel room with him. After only twenty minutes in the close quarters of his truck, she'd been *this* close to begging him to pull off to the side of the road so she could have her wicked way with him.

She could still feel the shivery vibes coiling in her spine as she recalled him coming to a stoplight, then turning to stare at her.

I want you.

He didn't have to say the words out loud. She simply knew it—and felt it. His eyes practically burned with intensity.

Goose bumps tickled her arms, heat filled her chest and—she still blushed to think about it—a tingling warmth grew between her thighs as she became aware of what he was thinking.

God help her, but she wanted him, too.

Slowly Connor had begun to grin, as if he could read her mind, damn him.

Then the signal changed to green. He'd turned away from her and stepped on the gas. And the moment was gone.

But he hadn't stopped grinning like a lunatic.

Maggie's first impulse had been to jump out of that truck and run as fast and as far as she could go. But she'd talked herself out of that plan, shook off her feelings and pulled herself together. She could handle this!

They had spent the rest of the ride making small talk, chatting about his mom, her grandfather, the goats, anything she could think of to keep herself from dwelling on Connor's sexy mouth, his dark unfathomable eyes, his impressive shoulders.

And she still thought she could avoid him for a whole week in the intimate confines of a hotel suite? Was she out of her mind? Maybe. But she'd already called the hotel twice to check on available rooms. There was nothing. In fact, there were no rooms anywhere in the area. She was stuck.

But on the other hand, maybe the hotel would have a few cancellations today.

During the ride, she had confessed to Connor, "Once we get to the hotel, I'm going to try one more time to see if there's another room available."

"Not ready to give up yet?"

"No," she said, and felt a twinge of pride. Why should she give up trying to stand on her own two feet?

He glanced at her sideways. "Fine. But you're doomed for disappointment. I have every intention of sharing the suite with you."

"But why?"

He shrugged. "I want to keep an eye on you. It's a big hotel. Anything could happen."

"What's that supposed to mean?" she demanded. "I'm perfectly capable of taking care of myself, Connor."

"I know," he said patiently, as if she might've mentioned it once or twice before. Well, maybe she had, but it bore repeating.

She continued. "I just think it's wrong for us to be…"

"Sharing a bed?" he said, finishing her sentence. "Living in such close proximity? Breathing the same air? What's the matter, Maggie? Don't think you can handle it?"

"I can handle it," she protested.

"Can you? Aren't you afraid I'll melt your resistance and have you begging for my body tonight?" He flashed her that cocky grin. "I don't blame you for being worried. Let's face it, I'm awesome. I'm smart, I'm wealthy, I'm hot, I'm, like, the perfect guy. It'll be a real challenge for you."

She burst out laughing. "Right. You wish."

Smiling agreeably, he took hold of her hand in what should've been a casual gesture, but it sent electric shock waves zipping up her arm and had her stomach muscles trembling with need.

"Look," he said. "We can check the room availability if you insist, but even if they do have something, I'd rather we stayed together. In case you forgot, you're my date for the week. You agreed to that, remember?"

"I remember." How could she forget when he kept reminding her? And she *had* agreed to abide by his terms of the deal. Not that she'd had a choice, but it was too late to whine about it now. She sighed inwardly. He was just doing this to get back at her for leaving him ten years ago. He wanted to teach her a lesson. Fine. She could handle his little power trip. If staying with him meant that she would obtain the loan money, she was willing to do whatever it took.

That money was vital to her future.

As she crossed the hotel lobby, it was clear to Maggie that as long as she kept looking for a way out of their deal, Connor would fight her at every step. And she wouldn't put it past him to fight dirty, either. So was it worth her time and energy to keep trying to pitch a flag on this hill? Probably not.

But that still didn't mean she would sleep with him, no matter what he might be planning.

After confirming with the reservationist at the front desk that there were definitely no rooms available, Maggie needed coffee. She was in luck; there was a coffee kiosk right in the lobby. After slugging down a medium café latte, she again felt capable of adult conversation.

She spent the rest of the morning on the lower level of the conference center, checking in with the judging officials. It took a long time to go through all the necessary paperwork and get her cases of beer unloaded and marked. She didn't mind the rules and procedures. The officials wanted to make sure that the so-called blind tastings were carried out in a forthright and aboveboard manner.

It was common knowledge that anyone who won a festival award was practically guaranteed thousands of additional orders along with a tremendous amount of free advertising and marketing. So to ensure that each entrant's beverages received a fair review, the festival operators went to great lengths to set up numerous firewalls and protective measures.

Maggie had no idea security would be so elaborate. Because of her need to remain anonymous, she'd managed to personally avoid the contest circuit for the past three years, so she almost laughed when she was instructed to step behind a thick red drape in order to shield herself from the curious eyes of other contestants in line.

Once behind the privacy curtain, she was greeted by a tall, beefy fellow in a tight black T-shirt who wore a name tag that read Johnny. He looked like a bouncer. "Got your copy of the entry form?"

Maggie handed him the multipage form and waited while he checked off boxes on a sheet of paper clipped to an official-looking clipboard.

"You're with Redhead Brewery?" he asked in a low voice to avoid being overheard.

"Yes," she whispered. The paranoia was contagious.

"I've never heard of Redhead Brewery and I've never seen you around here."

"It's a division of Taylor James," she said defensively, and was proud of herself for thinking fast to invoke the false name she'd used recently.

"Yeah?" Johnny looked impressed. "I love his stuff." He turned to the table next to him and sifted through one of many storage boxes filled with thick, sealed envelopes. He finally found the one he wanted and pulled it out. "Okay, I gotcha."

"Good," Maggie murmured, relieved.

Johnny glanced at her, took in her long red hair tied back in a ponytail and nodded. "Redhead Brewery. Now I get it. So what're you? Chief Executive Redhead?"

"That's right," Maggie said with a smile.

Johnny grinned as he leaned forward. "Okay, Red, here's the deal. You got three beers entered in the Small Brewery category. Tell me if these are the right names." He read off the quirky names of her pale ale, amber and lager.

"Yes, those are mine," Maggie said.

"Good." He opened the envelope and pulled out three index cards with printing on one side. "These are the official numbers the judges will use to review your entries. No names. Just numbers."

She watched him take a thick marker and write the corresponding numbers on each of her cases of beer.

Then he handed the index cards to her. "Don't let anybody see those cards, got it? We wouldn't want anything to compromise the outcome."

"Got it."

"I'm Johnny," the guy said, tapping his name tag as if she hadn't seen it before. "You got problems, you come see me."

She picked up her tote bag and purse. "Okay, thanks."

"Hold on, Red," he said, grabbing her arm. "I want to see you put those cards away where nobody else can see them." He wiggled his eyebrows at her, adding, "We don't want someone voting for you just because you're pretty."

"What? No." She whirled around to see if anyone had overheard him, then felt a chill skitter up her spine as she realized what she was doing. She was looking for her ex-husband! Alan used to freak out whenever anyone complimented her. He would accuse her of flirting and tell her she was turning into a whore. It wasn't fun. But good grief, she'd been away from him for three years. Enough already.

Would she ever be a normal person again? The thought depressed her, but she took in a few deep breaths and managed to work up a warm smile for Johnny as she slipped the cards into her purse. "Thanks, Johnny. I appreciate your help."

"You bet," he said, then jerked his head in the direction of the exit. "Now get outta here. And have a nice day."

Three hours later, Maggie sat on the sunny lobby level near the coffee kiosk. She had no idea where Connor was or when he would text their room number to her. But she figured she had enough time to enjoy her vanilla latte before she had to face the real challenge of the week: Connor MacLaren.

She'd had a busy day already. After signing in with Johnny at the judges' hall, she'd spent over an hour touring the huge convention floor, watching dozens of volunteers at work setting up booths, arranging kegs and glasses and signage. There was a band stage and a dance floor set up at one end of the room. The spacious beer garden overlooked the stage. The energy and excitement were infectious and she thought about volunteering next year.

After a while, she'd found an empty conference room, where she sat and studied the judges' guidelines again. Then she pored over the official program, highlighting the seminars she hoped to attend during the week. As she got up to leave, four brewpub owners walked in and she ended up having a spirited conversation with them about the industry and everything that was good and bad about it. Maggie had walked out in a cheery mood, feeling as though she was on her way to becoming part of a warm, friendly community.

As she had approached the escalator, another man joined her, grinning as they both stepped on the moving stairway at the same time.

"Enjoying yourself?" he asked.

"Yes, I am," Maggie said as she studied him briefly. He was nice looking in a passive, nonthreatening way. "I'm Maggie Jameson."

"Nice to meet you, Maggie." He gave her hand a hearty handshake. "I'm Ted Blake. I haven't seen you around the festival before. Are you in the business or just visiting?"

"This is my first time at the festival. I run my own microbrewery and I've entered some of my beers in the competition."

"How many workers do you have?"

She was a little taken aback by the direct question, but then figured he was just making friendly conversation. After all, they were all here to share information and grow the industry. "I'm it, for now."

"That's got to be hard."

"I enjoy it."

"What about your sales force?"

She frowned a little. "It's just me."

"Huh." He handed her a business card. "When you get tired of doing all the heavy lifting by yourself, give me a call."

She stared at his card, then looked up as they reached the main floor and stepped off the escalator. At that moment, Maggie noticed a pretty brunette staring fiercely at her from a booth a few yards away. The woman looked vaguely familiar—and she continued to glare directly at Maggie. Maggie was so surprised by the angry frown directed at her that she couldn't look away. After another long moment, the brunette tossed her hair back and turned away.

What in the world was that all about?

Nonplussed, Maggie glanced at her momentary companion. "It was nice meeting you, Ted."

"Hey, don't rush off," he cajoled.

But Maggie was desperate to spend a few minutes alone. "Sorry, but I'm meeting someone."

Now, as she sipped her vanilla latte by the wide plate-glass window, she tried to shake off the irritation she still felt from that woman's odd reaction to her.

Beyond the patio terrace and swimming pool area, the picturesque Point Cairn Marina bustled with activity. The small port had started life as a fishing village, and fishing was still a staple of the region. Fishing boats chugged their way back into the marina after a long day, pulling up to the docks to unload their catch of the day. Sailboats motored past on their way out to the ocean, where they would unfurl their sails and battle the strong winds and waves. In this part of Northern California, sailing was a sport for adrenaline junkies.

One sleek, teak-hulled yawl brought back memories of her father and his first sailboat. Maggie was ten years old when she and her mom and dad first started sailing together. It had been thrilling to skim across the water and feel the breeze ruffle her hair. That first summer on his new sailboat had been so much fun, with her father barking out orders and Maggie and her mom saluting and laughing as they trimmed the sails and adjusted the rigging according to his commands. They would sail to a small inlet where the waters were calm and the winds light. There they would drop anchor and have a picnic lunch. Once they even spent the night out on the water. It was magical.

But after that first season, her dad began to seek out rougher waters and more turbulent weather conditions. Maggie was ashamed to admit it, but she was too afraid to go with him after that. Her mother stopped going, too, and more than once, she tried to explain to Maggie why her father needed to seek bigger, more challenging adventures. White-water rapids, rock climbing, hiking the tallest mountains, parasailing. Her father tried it all and kept searching for wilder and more dangerous tests of will.

Maggie never did understand why being with her and her mother hadn't been enough for him.

Shaking off the melancholy, Maggie turned away from the marina view and glanced around the bustling lobby. The hotel was beginning to fill up with festival visitors and she wondered if she might recognize a friendly face or two. But she didn't see anyone she knew. Not yet, anyway. One of her goals for the week was to talk to and get to know as many people as she could manage.

Of course, she was also hoping to avoid any locals who might be less than happy to see her.

"Because I need something else to worry about," she muttered, shaking her head at the different directions her thoughts were taking her.

Since she wouldn't have much spare time later, Maggie pulled her schedule out of her purse and studied it one more time. Then she checked her judging number cards to make sure she hadn't lost them. They were still tucked inside her purse and she smiled as she pictured Johnny's stern look as he pretended to threaten her if she showed them to anyone. He might've been big and intimidating, but she knew he wouldn't hurt a flea. Johnny was the classic tough guy with a heart of gold.

She frowned as she recalled her own reaction to his offhanded remark about her being pretty. It annoyed her to know that she could still cringe at comments like that, a holdover from her years with Alan. Back then, if a man had complimented her, Alan would accuse her of having an affair with the guy. Once at a party, she and two other women had been joking about something. Later that night, Alan had wondered if the three of them might be forming a prostitution ring. She was so shocked she laughed at him. That had been a mistake. She learned quickly to avoid being friendly with other women and became an expert at discouraging attention from other men.

"Pitiful," she said, shaking her head. Even after three years back home, she was still living her life in the shadows, still trying so hard to be invisible that it came as a complete shock when a man noticed her, let alone complimented her.

But she refused to be depressed about it. She was so different from the woman she'd been even a year ago. She was happy to be at the festival and she was staying there with a gorgeous man, even though he had sort of blackmailed her into it. She had no intention of doing anything with him except sleep, preferably in a separate bed or on the couch. Still, it was exciting to be here.

Her phone beeped and she knew what that meant. Connor had sent her a text. Taking a deep breath, she read the message. Room 1292. Luggage is here and so am I. See you soon.

Suddenly she felt light-headed and wondered if it was caused by the caffeine or by Connor's message.

Did she really have to ask? It was Connor. Definitely.

Grabbing her tote bag and purse, she stood and tossed her empty coffee cup in the trash and headed for the elevator banks. Once in the elevator, she checked her purse again to make sure the number cards were still inside the zippered pocket.

Johnny would be happy to know how paranoid he'd made her.

Still, she was grateful for all the protective measures the festival had taken to ensure complete anonymity in the judging. Connor would never be able to figure out which entries were hers.

She frowned. She wasn't truly worried that he would try to sabotage her, was she? That wasn't his style, was it?

She brushed her concerns aside, but they creeped back in. How could she not worry just a little? Even though he'd been a perfect gentleman so far, they were still on shaky ground. Who knew what he really had in mind? Maybe he harbored a secret plan to humiliate her in front of the entire industry. Maybe he was going to all this trouble, only to destroy her fledgling reputation. Who could blame him? From his point of view, she'd apparently betrayed him all those years ago, left him behind with nothing but a broken heart.

It wasn't true, of course. He had been perfectly happy to break up with her. So why had he taken it so hard? At the time, Maggie had thought he was relieved to be rid of her. After all, he'd been the one to urge her to take that trip back east.

But she had obviously been wrong about his feelings. If her former high school friends were to be believed, Connor hadn't taken her departure well at all. So now she had to figure he might want to take her down a notch if the opportunity arose.

Would he stoop to searching out her secret judging numbers? Maybe he didn't even need to know them. Connor had worked for years in this business, tasting and testing and reformulating. And he'd been taking part in contests for all those years, too. He could probably decipher most of the different nuances of every brand and style of beer on the market.

Had he studied her particular formulas and techniques? He'd been following her progress for months—even though he'd thought he was following Taylor James, not Maggie. But didn't it stand to reason that after paying such intense attention to her techniques, Connor might be able to discern which beers were hers? And if he could, then why wouldn't he think about pushing her out of the running?

He certainly had strong motivation to sabotage her—and not just because she was his competition. No, Maggie figured that even after all this time, he might see this as a chance to get back at her for leaving him.

Revenge, after all, was a dish best served cold.

"Just stop," she muttered. She would drive herself crazy if she kept up that line of thinking. It would help if she could keep reminding herself that she had been with a good guy and a bad guy, and Connor was definitely one of the good guys. Besides, she had a bigger problem to deal with than the beer competition. Specifically, how to get through a whole week with Connor living in the same suite as her.

The elevator came to a quiet stop at the twelfth floor, otherwise known as the penthouse level. Maggie stepped out into the elegant hall and paused, taking in the parquet marble floor, the crystal chandeliers, the Louis XVI rococo furnishings. For a guy who preferred denim work shirts and blue jeans to an Armani suit, Connor MacLaren certainly liked to live in style. Maggie didn't know whether to be impressed or amused.

"Let the games begin," she muttered, and strolled toward the suite, once again wondering what in the world she'd gotten herself into.

* * *

Connor heard the water in the shower turn off and estimated that Maggie wouldn't be much longer. He reminded himself once again that he had shown excellent character earlier when he'd resisted the urge to follow her into the bathroom and join her in the shower like he'd wanted to.

While he waited, he glanced around the sitting room of the hotel suite. Earlier that day, in the hope that adding some romantic touches would somehow convince Maggie to fall into his bed, he'd arranged with the hotel florist and catering staff to bring bouquets of fragrant flowers and some champagne on ice to the room. Now soft jazz was playing in the background and a delectable dinner had been ordered. The kitchen staff was standing by to prepare and deliver it as soon as he placed the call.

This wasn't the first seduction scene Connor had arranged. If memory served, he'd done something similar the first time he'd made love with Maggie all those years ago. He could still remember the day as if it were yesterday. The lavish picnic on a deserted beach at sunset, aching desire, sweet hesitancy, shy touches, her giggles, his need, their bliss. For a while, anyway.

Connor ruthlessly shut off those flashes of memory and concentrated on his plans for right now. This time, he thought as he glanced around the room, at least he would know what he was doing.

As he double-checked that the champagne was properly chilled, he accepted that there would be no pretense of "making love" this time around. No, this time when he and Maggie got around to doing the deed, it would be good old-fashioned, sweaty, hard-driving sex—and plenty of it. That was the plan, anyway, despite Maggie's words of protest. The way she kissed him in his office told a different story. At least he hoped so.

And what about that searing hot gaze she'd cast his way

that morning in the truck? If that was any indication of her feelings, he figured it wouldn't be too hard to bring his plan to fruition. So to speak.

They both seemed to be on the same wavelength. And why not? After all, he mused, as he carried a large vase of stunning red roses over to the mantel, this wasn't their first rodeo together. They'd done this before. So why not do it again, for old times' sake? They were two consenting adults, right?

And in case she didn't see it that way, Connor figured the flowers and champagne would go a long way toward softening her attitude.

He didn't mind putting on a romantic show for a woman when the situation called for it, as long as it worked out in his favor. And yeah, by that he meant sex. He wasn't ashamed to admit that that was the bottom line.

Connor stared out the window at the sun setting over the ocean view and frowned. Was he starting to sound callous or deceptive? Because he wasn't that guy. He didn't expect Maggie to say yes simply because he was loaning her some money. He grimaced at the very thought. He would never make sex a condition for the loan, for Pete's sake. He didn't have to, he thought with a grin. His charm and persuasive abilities would take care of any qualms she might have.

Although why she would have qualms, he didn't know. She wanted him as badly as he wanted her, that much Connor knew. Maggie's expressions were still easy for him to read, so he figured he wouldn't have to work too hard to make it happen.

"This is a beautiful room."

He whirled around. Maggie stood near the doorway to the bedroom, using a towel to fluff her still-damp hair. She was dressed casually in a cropped T-shirt and a pair of those sexy yoga pants some women wore that fit like a second skin. Connor gave a brief prayer of thanks for that current fashion choice.

"I was in such a rush earlier," she murmured, and took her time meandering about, touching a knitted throw rug hanging off the sofa, studying the artwork, smelling the roses. "Oh, the flowers are gorgeous, aren't they?"

Connor couldn't help staring at her as she moved with supple ease around the room. Her feet were bare, her petite shoulders straight. Her hair, thick and healthy, became lighter and more lustrous as it dried. He could see the outline of her breasts as they rose and fell with each breath she took.

His groin tightened.

How had he forgotten how sexy her toes were? How perfect her skin was? To give himself some credit, he'd never forgotten her breasts.

As beautiful as she was, Maggie seemed more fragile now than when she was younger. She was quieter, too. Or maybe it just seemed that way because they were getting to know each other all over again. He would have to wait a few days to decide if that was true or not.

Only one thing marred the perfection of her face, and that was her eyes, where he caught the slightest hint of sadness that didn't seem to fade, even when she smiled.

He glanced down at her feet again, then rubbed his hand across his jaw when he realized what a complete fool he was. Damn it, he wanted her as he'd never wanted anyone before—except her, of course, all those years ago. At the same time, he wanted to lash out at her and demand to know why she'd left him, why she'd betrayed him, why she'd broken his heart ten years before.

But he would never say those words aloud. She didn't need to know how ridiculously vulnerable he was in her presence. Hell, she'd been driving him crazy ever since she walked into his office last week. He'd thought about her all week, at every hour, no matter where he was or what he was doing. She didn't have to be in the same room with him or, hell, the same city. He couldn't get her out of his mind. But he would. Once they'd slept together again, Connor would be able to rid himself of these lingering feelings and get on with his life.

Maggie had circled the room and was now standing in front of the ice bucket holding the bottle of expensive champagne. She turned to him. "What's this for?"

"Us," he said, crossing the room to open the bottle. "Champagne. I thought we'd celebrate."

She blinked in surprise. "Celebrate what?"

He thought quickly. "This is the first time you've attended the festival, right?"

"Right."

"So we're celebrating."

"Okay. Let me get rid of this first." She took the damp towel back to the bathroom and returned in seconds. "So, what's the plan tonight?"

"I thought we could dine here in the room." Connor pulled the chilled bottle out of the ice and wrapped it in a cloth. "Do you mind?"

"I don't mind at all. It sounds perfect."

"Good." He removed the metal cover and wire cage, then carefully twisted the cork until it popped. After filling two glasses with the sparkling liquid, he handed one to Maggie.

"Cheers, Mary Margaret."

"Cheers," she murmured, and took her first sip. "Mm, nice."

"I hope you still like steak," he said.

"I love steak."

"Good, because I've taken care of ordering dinner for us."

She swallowed too fast and began to cough. Setting

her glass down, she breathed in and out a few times and coughed to clear her throat.

"You okay?" he asked, ready to pound on her back if necessary.

"I'm fine." She folded her arms tightly across her chest and pinned him with an angry look. "You had no right to do that, Connor. I can order my own food and pay for it, too."

He shrugged. "I guess you could, but I already took care of it."

She stomped her foot. "How dare you?"

"Dial it back a notch, will you?" he said, his annoyance growing. "It's just dinner. Besides, how did you plan to pay for it? You came to me for money, remember?"

Her eyes widened as she clenched her teeth together. She looked about ready to scream, but seemed to swallow the urge and just stood there staring at him.

"What's the problem here, Maggie?"

Instead of answering him, she whirled around and paced, muttering under her breath. Connor could only hear every third word, but it didn't sound flattering to him. Abruptly she stopped in her tracks, inhaled and exhaled once, then again, and continued her pacing.

What in the world had just happened to her?

On her third pass, he grabbed her arm to stop her. "What the hell's wrong with you? I didn't order you gruel, for God's sake. Besides, you can order anything you want, you know that."

"Do I?" she asked.

Incredulous, he instantly replied, "Of course you do." Surprised by his own anger, he took a long, slow breath, then continued quietly. "But why should you? I ordered all your favorite foods. Steak, medium rare, baked potato with butter *and* sour cream, lightly grilled asparagus. Chocolate mousse for dessert. I thought you'd be happy. You used to love all that stuff."

She gaped at him for so long it was almost as if she was seeing him for the first time. Then she sucked in a big gulp of air as if she'd been underwater for too long. As she exhaled slowly, her anger seemed to deflate at the same time.

"You okay?" he asked, searching her face.

"Yes." She shook her head, clearly dismayed. "Yes. I'm fine. And I'm sorry, Connor. That was really stupid."

"No, just confusing," he said, flashing her a tentative smile.

Still breathing deeply as though she was centering herself, she ran her hands through her hair and then shook her head. Her eyes were clear now and she smiled. "Dinner, um, sounds great. You have a good memory. Those foods are still my favorites."

"Glad to hear it," he said cautiously, and handed her the glass of champagne she'd forgotten about. "But there's something I did that set you off. Tell me what it was so I don't do it again."

She took a healthy sip of champagne. "It's nothing you did. It's just something that I… Never mind." She walked to the window, then turned. "Just…thank you for ordering dinner. I know it'll be delicious."

"Oh, come on, Maggie," he said, losing patience. "After all this time, we can at least be honest with each other. Tell me what I did so I don't make the same damn mistake again."

She chewed her lower lip and Connor wondered if she might start crying. *Crap.* "Maggie, please don't cry. I'm sorry for…whatever I did."

"For goodness' sake, Connor, I'm not going to cry. And you didn't do anything. I just get a little carried away sometimes."

"If you say so."

"I do."

He watched her for another moment, then said lightly,

"Okay, I'm glad it's nothing I did. But I want you to know you've got the green light to yell or cry if you feel the need to."

"A green light? To cry?" She nodded, biting back a smile. "I appreciate that, but I have no intention of crying."

"You never know." He gave a worldly shrug. "Happens all the time."

She laughed. "Somehow I don't picture women bursting into tears around you."

"Not so much," he admitted, adding to himself, *Not ever.* The sophisticated women he'd dated over the past ten years would never dream of revealing their true emotions, let alone break down in tears. If for no other reason than it would ruin their expertly applied makeup.

And that was fine with him. Emotions could get messy and out of hand, and he wasn't interested in that. That's why, despite being a fairly casual guy with a laid-back style, he preferred to go out with worldly women who knew the score, who knew they could count on him for a great evening of dining and dancing, always followed by great sex, and that was it. What more could he ask for? No mess, no fuss.

"Tell you what." He took her arm and led her over to the sofa. "Come sit and relax. Enjoy your drink. There's no pressure here."

She did as he suggested and sipped her champagne. He sat down at the opposite end of the couch and she turned to him. "You must think I'm a fool."

He stared at her for a moment. It would be a mistake to get lost in those big brown eyes and that perfectly shaped mouth, but he wanted to. He really wanted to. Maybe later. For now, he wanted some answers. "I don't know what to think, Maggie, because you won't tell me."

She gazed at the bubbles in her glass, and Connor could tell her mind had gone a thousand miles away. Fine. She wouldn't reveal anything to him. And why should she? They weren't exactly friends anymore. She was only here because she needed the money. So what did that make them? Business partners? Hardly. Jailor and prisoner? Absolutely not, although she might look at things differently.

After another minute of silence, he figured he might as well send for dinner and reached for the telephone.

"My ex-husband," she began quietly, "also used to choose my meals for me. Among other things."

"Ah." Connor still wasn't clear about the problem, but he was glad she was finally talking. "Did he force you to eat liver or something?"

She laughed. A good sign. "No, he ordered what he thought I should eat. He didn't think I was capable of making my own decisions."

"Was he some kind of a health nut?"

"No. He was just convinced that he knew better than I did what I should be eating. And drinking. And wearing."

"Huh," he said, frowning. "Sounds like a control freak."

"Oh, *control freak* doesn't begin to describe him," she said, struggling to keep a light tone. "He made all my decisions for me. So when you said you ordered my dinner for me, I guess I flashed back to a different time and place and…well, sort of lost it."

"Sort of."

She reached over and touched his arm, gave it a light squeeze. "I'm sorry."

"Stop apologizing. I just wanted to know where that reaction came from. Now I know where I stand and we can move on. And I promise I won't make any more decisions for you."

She laughed for real this time and her eyes twinkled with humor. "Oh yes, you will."

He grinned. "You're probably right. But you can always punch me in the stomach if you don't agree."

"Thank you. You have no idea how much that means to me."

"Hmm." He rubbed his stomach. "I'm afraid to find out."

With a lighthearted chuckle, she held her glass out to his. "Cheers."

"Cheers," he said, clinking his glass against hers and then taking a drink. He was relieved to see her relaxed and smiling again and he wanted her to stay that way. So as much as his curiosity was gnawing at him, there was no way he would bring up the subject of her ex-husband again tonight. Besides being an obvious buzz kill, the guy sounded like a real jackass.

Okay, so the evening hadn't started out exactly as he'd planned, but that didn't mean it couldn't end up exactly where he wanted it to.

With Maggie in his bed.

Five

The dinner was fabulous, as Connor knew it would be. The steak was cooked to perfection, the chocolate mousse was drool-worthy and their conversation was relaxed with plenty of laughs and easy smiles. Connor had kept the champagne flowing and had consciously avoided any talk of ex-husbands and old betrayals.

Sated, he sat back in his chair and watched Maggie as she savored the last luscious spoonful of chocolate mousse. He'd enjoyed the dinner, too, but had found himself getting much more pleasure from observing her delight than from his own meal. Maybe too much pleasure, if the relentless surge of physical need that had grabbed hold of him was any measure to go by.

But what could he do about it? He was mesmerized by her luxuriant tumble of reddish-brown hair that floated over her shoulders and down her back. And her face, so delicately shaped and porcelain smooth, begged to be touched. Her lips were soft, full and voluptuous, and Connor's fervent desire to taste them again was driving him dangerously close to the edge.

He cursed inwardly. His famous self-control was slipping. He had to find a way to pull the reins in on his rampant libido. But how could he look away while Maggie still licked and nibbled at her spoon, lost in her own little world of chocolate mousse goodness, for God's sake?

She was killing him. He wouldn't survive another meal. Not until he'd had her in his bed.

Soon, he promised himself. Very soon. For now, he forced himself to stop watching her pink tongue darting and nipping at the spoon. Instead he glanced up and tried to appreciate the elegant and somber artwork on the wall while he shifted unobtrusively in his chair, carefully adjusting himself so she wouldn't notice the rather prominent bulge in his pants.

When he finally could speak in coherent syllables, he said, "So, I take it you enjoyed dinner?"

"Oh yes," Maggie murmured as she set down her spoon. "Delicious. Thank you, Connor."

"My pleasure." Connor was just glad she'd put down that damn spoon. One more lick and he would've been a dead man.

She lifted her teacup and took a sip, then set it down and smiled at him. "This has been so nice."

Nice? he thought. He was barely grasping hold of the edge of madness and she was having a tea party.

He needed to get a grip.

"Why don't we move over to the sofa?" he suggested, standing and reaching for her chair. "We can talk some more and you can finish your tea."

She hesitated a moment, then nodded. "Yes, all right."

They settled at their respective ends of the comfortable sofa. Maggie seemed a bit shy again, now that she didn't have the safe barrier of plates and food between them. But Connor kept the conversation light and she eased back into it.

Every time Connor thought about what Maggie had told him about her ex-husband, he felt more and more bemused. She hadn't been living the high life as he'd always assumed, and now he didn't know what to think. Really, though, how bad could it have been? The guy was worth millions. Should Connor feel badly for Maggie because the guy she ended up marrying turned out to be kind of a jerk?

After twenty minutes of safe conversation centered mostly on goats, beer, Angus and Deidre, Connor's mom, Maggie yawned. "It's been a long day and tomorrow will be a busy one. I think I'd better go to bed."

She stood and reached her arms up in a stretch that caused her shirt to tighten dangerously across her perfect breasts. Connor had to look away or beg for mercy.

After a minute, she relaxed, picked up her teacup and took it over to the dining table. Connor followed her, but before he could say anything or make a move, Maggie turned and stopped him with a firm hand against his chest.

"You got your way, Connor," she said. "I'm staying in the suite with you. Dinner was lovely, thank you, but I'm not going to sleep with you, so don't bother trying to make me."

"*Make* you?"

"That's right, don't try to talk me into anything." She folded her arms under her chest in a stubborn move that only accented her luscious breasts. "I'm not going to change my mind."

He held up both hands innocently. "I never expected you to."

"Yes, you did."

"No, Maggie. You're the one who keeps bringing it up."

"What? Me? No, I—"

"And frankly, I don't think it's a good idea."

Her eyes narrowed in suspicion. "You...don't think *what's* a good idea?"

"Sex," he said easily, though he was cringing on the inside. "Look, we had a nice evening, but as you said, tomorrow's going to be another long day, so I think we should call it a night."

She frowned. "You do."

"Yes, I do." He nodded calmly, mentally patting himself on the back for putting on this show of levelheadedness. "Look, you said it would be wrong and I'm agreeing with you."

"You're…agreeing with me. Okay. Good." It took her a moment, but finally she gave him a tentative smile. "Well, then, good night. Thank you again for a lovely evening."

He glanced down at her hand still pressed against his chest. "Good night, Mary Margaret."

"Oh." She whipped her hand away. "Okay, good night."

"Wait." With an innocent smile, he reached out and took hold of her arms. "I'll sleep better if I can have a good-night kiss. Just one. For old times' sake."

She gave him a look. "Oh, all right." Then she seemed to brace herself as she puckered up for a chaste kiss.

But instead of kissing her mouth, Connor bent his head and kissed her shoulder. Then he moved an inch and kissed the small patch of skin at the base of her neck.

She was gasping by the time he reached her jaw line. "What are you doing to me?"

He nibbled and kissed her ear, then whispered, "We're not sleeping together, no matter how much you beg me."

"Beg you?" She stretched her neck to give him more access to the pale smoothness of her skin. "This is crazy."

"I know," he murmured. "I wish you'd stop it."

"I'm not…"

But she couldn't seem to finish as he began licking each inviting corner of her mouth. When she moaned aloud, he pressed his lips to hers in an openmouthed kiss more erotic than anything he'd ever experienced. She was sweeter than chocolate and more intoxicating than the cognac they'd shared earlier.

He realized his mistake immediately, tried to keep the kiss light, but it was no use. He wanted her with the intensity of a red-hot sun, wanted to pull her down on the couch and touch her everywhere, from the tips of her sexy pink toenails to the top of her gorgeous red mane. And each place in between, too. He could do it, he knew. She was willing and wanted the same thing he did. And damn, he needed her now, needed to be inside her, to spread her shapely legs and press into her, sheathing himself in her dusky depths.

Damn it. He'd set up this whole evening to be a romantic interlude leading directly to sex. But despite her body pressed tightly against his, he knew she needed time to get used to being with him again. So why didn't he stop? He knew with every kiss that he was making things worse for himself. He'd go insane before much longer if he didn't put an end to this right now.

But then she moaned and he reconsidered, and somehow his hand moved to cup the soft swell of her breast. And a part of him felt as though he'd come home after being away a long time. He recognized the sweet roundness and wanted nothing more than to get lost in her, nothing more than to touch his tongue to her beaded nipples and hear the familiar sound of her little gasps and whispers of bliss.

And if he didn't stop now, he never would. With unearthly strength of will, he forced himself to end the kiss and pull away from her soft curves. And immediately missed the warmth.

He ran his hands up and down her toned arms, then squeezed them lightly, before taking another step back. The only reward for his good behavior was her look of dazed wonder. He wasn't sure it was worth his sacrifice, but it was too late to change his mind.

"Time for bed, Mary Margaret." He wrapped his arm lightly around her shoulder and led her into the bedroom, where he gathered up a blanket and pillow.

She dropped onto the bed and watched him.

He smiled tightly and held up his hand in a sign of farewell, as though he were a soldier heading for battle. "Good night. Sweet dreams."

"G-good night, Connor. Thank you."

He walked out of the room and closed the door behind him.

So much for tactical retreats, Connor thought the next morning, after he tried to roll over in bed and slid off the couch onto the floor instead.

"Damn it," he grumbled, rubbing his elbow where it smacked against the coffee table. "Where the hell...oh yeah."

After a minute, he managed to pull himself up off the floor and sat on the couch with his elbows on his knees, head resting in his hands. As his brain slowly emerged from the fog of sleep, he played back the events of last night that had ultimately led to him sleeping on the couch.

At the time, it had appeared to be a brilliantly strategic move. After several long, hot kisses, he had no doubt Maggie had been tempted to give in to her desires and join him in bed. But no, Connor had decided that rather than moving in for the kill, he would leave her wanting more. His theory, which clearly needed work, was that with any luck, tonight she would be seducing him instead of the other way around.

It had seemed like such a smart idea at the time.

"Idiot," he muttered, scratching his head. "How's that strategy working out for you?" Cursing under his breath, he gathered up the blanket and pillow off the couch.

He entered the bedroom and found Maggie sound asleep. So she was still enjoying a restful night's sleep while he was wide awake and whining in misery. Glaring at her, all peaceful and snug in their comfortable bed, Connor vowed that it wouldn't happen again. There was no way he was sleeping anywhere else tonight but in this bed—with Maggie tucked in right next to him.

He quietly rummaged around in one of the drawers until

he found his gym shorts and sneakers and slipped them on, then took off for a bracing run along the boardwalk.

Halfway through the run, despite his determination to take in the crisp ocean breezes and enjoy the clear blue sky, he caught himself grumbling again. Uttering a succinct oath, he forced himself to shove the surly thoughts away and look on the bright side. So maybe last night hadn't gone exactly according to plan. It didn't matter. He was a patient man and he knew he would have Maggie in his bed soon. He'd stoked not only his fire, but hers, as well. She might've slept soundly but he was willing to bet he'd been a major player in her dreams.

Tonight, it was going to be different. He had all day to convince her that she wanted him as much as he wanted her. Maybe more.

Grinning now, he thought about Maggie and how she'd nearly succumbed to her own needs last night. It wouldn't take much to bring her to that point again. Hell, he loved a good challenge and she was nothing if not challenging.

He would prevail, of that he had no doubt. And with that happy thought in mind, he jogged back to the hotel to take a shower and get ready for the long day ahead.

Maggie heard the suite door close and checked the bedside clock. Connor had mentioned the night before that he might go running this morning, so Maggie figured she had at least a half hour to get ready for the day. She jumped out of bed and took a quick shower, then dried her hair and dressed in black pants and a deep burgundy sweater. She slipped her feet into a comfortable but attractive pair of flats because she had no intention of walking around the convention floor all day in heels. If Connor insisted that she dress up for dinner, she would come upstairs and change into her killer pumps. Otherwise, she was going for comfort.

Last week he'd made it clear that their week would be

more business-oriented than fun-filled, so she shouldn't be bothered to pack any blue jeans or work boots to wear this week. She mused that it should've bugged the heck out of her that Connor had dared to tell her what to wear, but after he'd explained what they'd be doing, it made sense.

But she'd still slipped one old pair of jeans and sneakers into her suitcase, on the off chance that she'd have some time by herself during the week.

The good news was that Connor would be forced to suffer in his business attire as much as she would, since, based on everything she knew about him, he lived in denim work shirts and blue jeans every day, too.

Maggie wrote a note for Connor telling him she would be waiting somewhere near the coffee kiosk downstairs. Then she grabbed her lightweight blazer and left the suite.

Forty-five minutes later, her heart stuttered in her chest at the sight of the smiling, handsome man walking right toward her. She could get used to that sight, she thought wistfully, but just as quickly, she banished the thought away. Getting used to having Connor around would be a major league mistake and she'd be smart to remember that. They were only spending this week together because she was desperate for money and he seemed to want to teach her a lesson.

Still, it couldn't hurt to look her fill.

He was so…formidable, despite his clean-cut outfit of khakis worn with a navy V-neck sweater over a white T-shirt. He should've come across more like the boy next door. Instead he looked dangerous, powerful, intense as he prowled confidently across the room like a sexy panther stalking his mate. Maggie noticed other women giving him sly looks as he passed, and part of her wanted to stand up and shout, "He's mine!"

But he wasn't *hers,* Maggie reminded herself, and he never would be again. The thought depressed her, but she pushed it aside instantly. She could be sad and whiny about that later. For now, for this week, she vowed to enjoy every minute of her time with him.

After convincing Connor to have a quick breakfast of coffee and a muffin, Maggie and he walked across the hotel to the convention entrance. She was surprised to see the convention floor packed with people, even though the festival was not yet open to the general public.

These first few days were mainly devoted to programs and workshops designed to appeal to those industry professionals in attendance. Maggie was looking forward to attending several of them and had them highlighted in her program booklet.

But already, hundreds of booths were doing a brisk business serving tastes of every type of beer and ale imaginable and selling all sorts of souvenirs. It was a clear sign that the beer-making community enjoyed partaking of its own products.

As they strolled through the crowd, Connor would occasionally take her hand in his to prevent them from being split up. Maggie tried to remember it didn't mean anything, but his touch was potent and unsettling. Each time, he seemed to set off electrical currents inside her that zinged through her system and left her dizzy and distracted.

It didn't help that every few minutes, Connor would run into someone he knew. He would stop and talk and introduce Maggie, assuring his friends that she was destined to be the next superstar in their industry.

Maggie wasn't quite sure what to think of Connor's kind words and she had absolutely no idea what to do with all the positive energy being directed at her from his friends and business associates. She smiled and chatted and appreciated it all, of course. Who wouldn't? These people could open important doors for her that had been closed and locked until now.

But it was confusing. Was this Connor's way of teaching her a lesson? Of getting back at her for breaking his heart ten years ago? If so, it was diabolical. He was killing her with kindness, the beast!

To divert herself, she concentrated on the swarm of festival attendees and the cheerful babble of twenty different conversations going on around her. She warned herself that if she thought it was crowded now, just wait until the weekend. The place would be packed wall to wall with people, and the noise level would be overwhelming with rock bands playing and even more demonstrations and activities going on. Maggie couldn't believe she was actually looking forward to the crush of humanity.

Connor continued to run into friends and associates every few seconds. It was amazing to see how many people he knew. But of course, he'd always been outgoing and charming. His mom used to say that Connor had never met a stranger, and it was true. Everyone he met became a friend.

He persisted in pulling Maggie over to introduce her to each new person, and she began to relax and enjoy herself, grateful that he would think to include her in both his business and his personal conversations with people. She hadn't expected it. Frankly, she was still trying to convince herself that she knew him, knew he was not the type to resort to sabotage. But was that true? May not be, but it didn't seem to be on his agenda today. At least, not yet.

And the fact that he was being so generous and inclusive and kind to her made it all the more difficult to cling to her determination not to sleep with him.

Not that she would have sex with him simply because he'd given her a few good business contacts. No way. Her gratitude didn't extend *that* far. But it was getting more and more difficult to ignore the fact that Connor MacLaren was simply a thoughtful, honorable man, a good person, just as he'd been when she knew him ten years ago. He hadn't changed.

It was Maggie who had changed. Who would have guessed that when she and Connor broke up, she was simply trading one set of risks for another worse set? The result was that now, after ten years, she was more guarded, more tentative, more jumpy. All those years with Alan and his mother had not been good for her.

But those years were over. It was all in the past and she was moving forward, living in the present and planning for the future. She was doing okay.

The fact that she'd stepped out of her comfort zone, taken the risk and faced down Connor MacLaren in his own office a week ago was something to be proud of. And, she thought as she gazed around at the festival crowd, she was actually out having fun. It was such a dramatic change from the way she'd been three years ago that she wanted to jump up and give a little cheer. Go, Maggie, go!

She smiled to herself. Good thing nobody was monitoring her goofy thoughts.

"Maggie," Connor said, interrupting her meanderings. "Come meet Bill Storm, one of the top-selling beer makers in the country."

"Aw, hell, boy," the older man drawled. "I'd be the *very* top if it wasn't for y'all and your MacLaren's Pride."

Maggie smiled at the man, who had what was quite likely the world's largest mustache and a personality to go with it.

She shook his hand. "Hello, Mr. Storm."

"Call me Bill," he said jovially. "Mr. Storm is my old man."

"Thanks, Bill."

"Now, Connor here tells me that some of the pale ales

you've been producing might just be the hottest beers to hit the market in years." Bill scratched his head in thought. "Don't mind me being a little skeptical, but I can see with my own eyes what your actual appeal to him might be."

Suddenly wary, she glanced at Connor, who merely smiled at his friend's good-natured teasing. Maggie decided that the old guy meant no offense and turned back to Bill with her business card in her hand. "I'll be glad to give you a personal tasting of my latest beers and ales tomorrow."

"And I'll be glad to take you up on that, Maggie." He handed her his business card, too, and Maggie slipped it into the pocket of her tote bag. Then Bill drew Connor into a more personal conversation about a mutual competitor and after a minute, Maggie decided to wander around a bit.

She stopped at several booths to check out the competition and met so many friendly beer makers and brewpub operators that she was reminded of something her father had once told her. The beer-making community was famously close-knit and friendly and helpful toward one another. Yes, there was plenty of competition, but they generally cheered their rivals on and supported each other.

At the fourth booth she came to, she stopped and stared and then began to laugh.

"That's the reaction I get most of the time," the guy said cheerfully.

His three featured beers had been given the silliest names she'd seen in a long time.

Maggie had learned early on that one of the joys of running a small craft brewery was coming up with a colorful name for the final product. Some brewers went for shock value, others enjoyed grunge and still others tried for humor.

The names of Maggie's beers were rather tame compared to some. This year she'd chosen the names of famous redheads to call attention to her Redhead brand. Her three competition entries were Rita Hayworth, Maureen O'Hara and Lucy Ricardo.

The barrel-chested, sandy-haired man running the booth turned out to be the brewery owner, who introduced himself as Pete. "Would you like a glass of something?"

"It's a little early for me to be tasting," she said with a smile. "But I was wondering who came up with these names of yours."

Pete beamed with pride. "My three sons come up with most of our names."

"Must be nice to have sons," she said. "Do they help you out with the brewing?"

"No way," Pete said, laughing. "Not yet, anyway. They're all under the age of seven. They're the creative arm of the company."

"Ah, that makes sense," she said, nodding, and picked up one of the bottles. "I was wondering what inspired you to name this one Poodle's Butt."

"That came from the warped mind of my five-year-old, Austin. But don't be fooled. Poodle's Butt is a fantastic, full-bodied beer with a hint of citrus and spice that I think you'll find unique and flavorful—if you can get past the name."

She chuckled. "I love the name. I'll try and come back for a taste later today." She pointed to another bottle. "Now, what about Snotty Bobby Pale Ale?"

"Bobby's my oldest. He came up with that idea last year when he had a cold. Laughed himself silly over his idea," Pete said, then added sheepishly, "I did, too. Guess they got their sense of humor from me."

Maggie patted his arm. "You should be very proud."

"I really am."

"Hey, Maggie."

She turned and came face to face with the quirky man she'd met the first day. "Oh, hello, Ted."

He flashed her a crooked grin. "I hope you thought about what I told you the other day."

"I really don't think I—"

"There you are," a voice said from close behind her.

Maggie whirled around and found Connor standing inches away. Her stomach did a pleasant little flip. "Hi."

But Connor wasn't looking at her. He was staring over her shoulder at Ted.

"Have you met Ted?" Maggie asked. "He's…" She turned, but Ted was gone. She spied him halfway across the room, jogging through the crowd.

"That was weird," she murmured.

"How well do you know that guy?" Connor asked bluntly.

"Not well at all."

"You might want to keep it that way."

Someone cleared his throat behind her. "Oh, Pete! Connor, have you met Pete? He owns Stink Bug Brewery."

Connor and Pete shook hands and talked for a minute or two, and then Connor grabbed her hand. "We should go. I want to check the judging schedule downstairs."

Maggie promised Pete she'd return later; then she and Connor left to find the escalators. Once they were descending to the lower level, Connor let go of her hand and glanced around. "This place is going to be packed by Friday."

"Isn't it fabulous?"

"Fabulous?" He gave her a curious smile. "Most people would be annoyed with all the crowding. But not you."

"This is my first festival, after all."

"Right. No wonder you're so excited." They stepped off the escalator and walked the long corridor toward the judges' hall. "So all this time you were entering competitions under your Taylor James name, you never actually showed up for any of the awards?"

She shook her head. "Not once."

"Why not?"

She really didn't want to have this conversation, but she owed him an answer, even if it was lame. "I'm shy."

He snorted a laugh. "You've never been shy a day in your life. What's the real story?"

Back when he knew her, no, she hadn't been shy. But over the years with Alan, she had learned to become invisible. She couldn't say that, though, so she tried to keep it simple. "Things change. I'd been away for so many years, and by the time I got back home, I didn't really know anyone anymore. Some old friends had left town. New people had taken their place. You know how it is. So I wasn't as sure of myself as I used to be. Especially when it came to competing in this business."

"But your father ran a brewpub. I remember he was always winning medals. You must know you'd be welcomed wherever went."

"If only that were true." She smiled reflectively.

"Okay, even if nobody knew you, you've got this business in your blood. You had to know that your product was excellent. Seems like you'd want to show up in person and get the accolades."

"You're right, I should've," she admitted, "but I didn't. My confidence was pretty low, especially after a few run-ins with people in town. It made me realize I wasn't ready to take on the general public, so my cousin Jane and her boyfriend agreed to attend the competitions on my behalf."

"What run-ins?"

Maggie cringed inwardly. Leave it to Connor to hone in on that key detail. She hadn't meant to blurt it out like that and she was wondering how to explain herself when they were interrupted.

"Hey, Red, is that you?"

Maggie turned and saw Johnny, the muscleman she'd met at yesterday's check-in.

"Hi, Johnny," she said, smiling. "Do you know Connor MacLaren?"

"Aw, hell," Johnny said with a grin. "Of course I do. How you doing, man?"

"Hey, Johnny." The two men shook hands. Then Connor looked at Maggie. "I'm going to head inside the hall for a minute to check the schedule."

"I'll wait out here."

"I won't be long."

He took off and Maggie chatted with Johnny for another minute until he had to get back to his line of people. Then she began to browse the long tables that had been set up to display the hundreds of promotional gadgets and giveaways. There were flyers, as well, and booklets that described the latest seminars and vendor products that might be useful to the industry professionals attending the festival.

She picked up a few clever gadgets and grabbed some flyers that looked interesting. Five minutes later, she glanced up and saw Connor waving at her as he exited the door at the far end of the judges' room.

Just as Maggie started walking down the corridor to meet him, three attractive women approached Connor from the opposite direction. There was a loud, feminine shriek and all three began to flutter and buzz around him. "Connor MacLaren! I thought it was you!"

"Ooh, it is Connor!" the blonde said. "Hey, you! You're looking good."

Maggie recognized the blonde as Sarah Myers, one of her best friends from high school. Sarah was also the first person to turn on Maggie when she returned home.

"Hi, Connor," the second woman said, and wound her arm around his. "I was hoping we'd see you here this week."

"Hi, Connor," the brown-haired woman said. She seemed more shy than the other two and as she got closer, Maggie recognized her. She was the angry woman who had stared at her the first day of the festival. The one who had glowered and glared and frowned, then flipped her hair and walked away.

And now she was staring at Maggie again. Maggie had an urge to rub her arms to ward off the chill.

Connor nodded at the brunette. "Hey, Lucinda. Are you working today?"

"No." Ignoring Maggie now, she grinned up at Connor. "Jake gave me the day off and we decided to check out the festival before it gets too crowded."

Did she work for MacLaren? Maggie wondered. If so, it was no wonder she wasn't quite as forward with Connor as her two friends were.

Sarah looked up at the Judges Only sign over the doorway. "Oh, hey, are you one of the judges? That's so cool!"

Maggie's stomach did a sharp nosedive. She felt ridiculous just standing there thirty or forty feet away from them, but she had no intention of joining the group and watching Connor be devoured by drooling groupies. There was no reason to be so annoyed. She had no claim on him, but that didn't seem to matter to her topsy-turvy emotions. She whipped around and took off in the opposite direction, praying that Connor hadn't seen her rapid retreat.

Maggie walked quickly, skirting the crowd until she reached Johnny's check-in line. She had resigned herself to the fact that she would eventually run into some familiar faces from town, but she didn't think it would happen until the weekend when the festival was opened to the public. Just her luck that Sarah and her posse had decided to show up early.

She slipped between the short queue of people waiting for Johnny and made her way farther down the hall to the ladies' room.

It was blessedly empty. Maggie stepped inside one of the stalls and locked the door. She leaned her forehead against the cold steel door and wondered how long she would have to stay in here. She felt like a desperate escapee trapped in here, but at least she was safe.

Safe?

"For goodness' sake, lighten up," she scolded herself aloud. Those silly women out there couldn't hurt her.

But they *could* hurt her, that was the problem. And she knew they would be more than happy to attack her again, only this time they would have an audience. Namely, Connor.

"They can only hurt you if you *let* them," she whispered. That was what the clinic counselor had told her a few years ago. Maggie knew those words were true, but knowing the truth hadn't made it any easier to ignore the taunts.

Maggie pounded her fist against the stall door. Damn it, wasn't ten years enough time to suffer for the presumed sins she'd committed against her high school boyfriend? Couldn't they behave like adults?

Even as she thought it, she had to laugh, since hiding in the bathroom wasn't exactly a grown-up move. She had to face this. Port Cairn was her home again and she couldn't spend all of her time running from people she'd once been friends with. Maggie had to find a way to convince Sarah to call a truce.

She would get to work on that right away, she thought with a soft laugh, as soon as she stopped shivering like a scared pup in this cold tiled bathroom. She wasn't exactly dealing from a place of strength at the moment.

She hated this feeling of shame. After three years of hard work and trial and error, she had accomplished so much and built an excellent reputation for herself. She should've been able to face her detractors with poise and confidence. But none of her achievements meant anything, as long as she was hiding in a bathroom stall like a sniveling coward.

"Not a pretty picture," she muttered, and with a defiant shake of her head, she straightened her shoulders. All it took was a little guts and determination to walk out of here with her head held high. And she would. Any minute now. It wasn't as if she was procrastinating or anything. But with the restroom still empty, this would be the perfect time to call and check in with her grandfather.

Pulling her phone out, she pushed Speed Dial and seconds later, Grandpa answered.

"Hi, Grandpa, it's Maggie."

"There's my sweet lass," he said, his Scottish brogue sounding stronger than she remembered. "Are ye having a bang-up time of it?"

"Best time ever," she lied. "Connor knows so many people and I've already made a lot of new contacts. Everyone is so nice and there's so much to see and do."

"Ah, that's lovely to hear, now."

"I miss you, Grandpa."

"Now, there's no need," he said. "I'm right here as always, tending to me darlings."

"Have you seen Deidre?" Maggie asked, anxious to make sure that Connor's mom had been stopping by.

"She interrupts me on an hourly basis," he grumbled.

"Good," Maggie said firmly. "I'm glad she's taking care of you."

"She's a good cook," he muttered. "I'll give her that much."

"She's a great friend."

"Yes, yes," he said impatiently, clearly not pleased that he'd been assigned a *babysitter*. "Now, Deidre mentioned that Connor's taking you to a fancy dance party. When is that?"

"It's Friday night, but I'm not going, Grandpa. You know I hate to dance. I didn't even bring a formal dress to wear."

"Ah, lass. You used to love to dance."

"Not so much anymore."

"You go to the dance," Grandpa insisted. "Connor deserves to dance with his beautiful girl."

"He'll have to live with the disappointment," she muttered, and quickly changed the subject. "How are Lydia and Vincent doing?"

"Och, they're randy as two goats."

She chuckled. "Grandpa, they *are* goats."

But he was already laughing so hard at his little joke that he began to cough.

"Grandpa, drink some water. You're going to choke."

"I'm fine," he said, but his voice was scratchy and he coughed another time or two. "Och, I haven't laughed like that in years. You're a tonic for me, Maggie."

She smiled. "I really do miss you, Grandpa."

"You'll be home soon enough, lass, soon enough," he said. "I'm pleased that you're getting out and about. You take some time and have fun with your Connor. And drink plenty of beer. It's good for you."

"I know, Grandpa. I love you."

"You're a good lass," he said softly, and Maggie understood it was his version of *I love you*.

They ended the call and Maggie sat and stared at the phone for a few seconds before she realized her eyes were damp. She wiped them dry; then with more resolve than courage, she left the stall, exited the bathroom and stepped out into the corridor.

"Maggie!"

She glanced around and spotted Connor waving at her from halfway down the football-field-length hallway. She didn't see any of the women with him, thankfully, so she waved and walked toward him. He met her midway.

"Where the hell have you been?" he asked.

"You looked busy a few minutes ago, so I went to use the bathroom and then called my grandfather."

"How's he doing?"

"He sounded fine. Your mom's already been there a bunch of times, so I know he's well looked after."

"Good." He slipped his arm around her shoulder, out of habit or companionship or something more significant, Maggie couldn't tell. But it felt so good to be this close to him. She breathed in the hint of citrus-and-spice aftershave, reveled in the protective warmth, loved that they fit together so perfectly, even if it was just for this brief moment. For so many years, she'd been unwilling to admit to herself that she had missed him, missed these moments of closeness with him. Life with her ex-husband had never been warm or cozy. Just cold. She shivered at the memory.

"Hey, Connor, over here."

They both turned and spotted Connor's two brothers coming their way with Lucinda, the same woman Maggie had seen with Sarah and her friend a few minutes ago. The same woman who couldn't seem to keep from frowning at her. Now she was holding a notebook and pen and didn't look happy about it. Had the brothers corralled her into doing some work? Probably so. That would explain her sour expression. Or maybe it was Maggie's own presence, she mused, but briskly brushed that thought away.

Connor quickly slid his arm away and Maggie felt foolishly bereft without his touch.

"Hey, guys," Connor said.

"You go ahead and talk to them," Maggie urged Connor. "I'm going up to the convention floor to look around some more."

"Stick around. You know my brothers." Connor grabbed her hand to keep her close by.

Maggie had a bad feeling about this little reunion, but she stayed with him and tried to think good thoughts.

"Is that Maggie Jameson?" Ian said as they got closer.

"Sure is," Connor said cheerfully.

"Hello, Maggie," the woman said tonelessly.

Maggie tried to smile. "Hi. It's Lucinda, right? You're Sarah's cousin. I remember you from high school. It's nice to see you."

Lucinda's lips twisted wryly, as though she didn't quite believe Maggie's words. "It's been a long time."

"Yes, it has," Maggie said, recalling more about the woman as they spoke. Lucinda had been a few years younger than Sarah, but she used to hang around with the group once in a while.

"I work for MacLaren now," she said, her tone proudly confrontational.

Maggie blinked. Lucinda made it sound like a challenge. As if she really meant to say, *These are my men. You keep your hands off.* Frankly, Maggie couldn't blame her. If Lucinda believed her cousin Sarah, she probably accepted the story that Maggie had destroyed Connor. Now she wasn't about to allow this witch to get near his brothers.

Jake and Ian exchanged glances and Maggie suddenly had a whole new reason for running again. They looked even less happy to see her than Lucinda did.

Naturally, Connor's brothers were aware that she'd left town all those years ago and probably assumed, as Lucinda and Sarah and everyone else in town seemed to, that she'd left him with a crushed and broken heart. If the accusations of Sarah and her other high school pals were the common wisdom around Point Cairn, namely, that Maggie had betrayed Connor with another man, then Jake and Ian most likely hated her as much as her old friends did.

So this would be fun.

"Hi, Ian. Hi, Jake," she said, trying to be upbeat. "It's good to see you both."

"Yeah, good to see you, too, Maggie," Ian said carefully. "How are you enjoying the festival?"

"I'm having a great time."

"Oh yeah? Did you enter something in the competition?"

"Yes, I've got three entries."

As she spoke to Ian, Jake leaned in to say something to Connor. Connor laughed, but Jake did nothing but stare stone-faced at Maggie.

She tried to block Jake from her line of sight as she attempted to continue the casual conversation with Ian, but it was impossible. She realized she could no longer stomach this level of judgmental scrutiny. Even Ian, who was at least willing to talk to her, was emitting the same reproachful vibes as Jake.

She reached out and touched Connor's arm to get his attention. "I—I've just remembered something I have to do upstairs. You can text me when you're finished down here and tell me where you want to meet."

"Wait," he said. "I'll only be a—"

But she couldn't wait. She had to go. She turned and walked away as fast as she could move, leaving the Mac-Laren brothers and their silent but palpable condemnation behind.

Six

Baffled, Connor watched Maggie dash off the convention floor. The urge to follow her was strong, but first he turned on Jake. "What just happened here?"

Jake shrugged. "Guess she didn't want to hang around."

"Don't pull that crap with me. You were freaking her out with your, whatever you call it, *evil eye* thing. And I don't appreciate it."

"You're awfully defensive," Jake said, standing his ground. "I thought you were never going to speak to her again. What changed your mind?"

"I grew up." Fuming, Connor glanced down the hallway. "That was over ten years ago, for God's sake. Let it go. And besides, you're the one who told me to bring a date this week."

"I was hoping you might bring someone who everyone could get along with."

"You could've asked me, Connor," Lucinda said.

Connor ignored her and frowned in frustration at his brother. "I thought you always liked Maggie."

"Well, sure, I liked her, until she screwed you over so badly that you could barely drag your ass out of bed for, like, a year."

"That's not true."

"Truer than you'd like to believe. Maybe that time was fun for you, but it wasn't for me. Or Ian, or Mom. Maggie ripped your heart out, man. We didn't think you'd ever recover. And I don't want to see it happen again."

Even if Jake's recollection was skewed, Connor could at least try to be grateful for his concern.

He suddenly realized that Lucinda was listening avidly to things he'd rather not share with anyone outside his family. With a tight smile, he said, "Hey, Lucinda, I thought Jake gave you the day off. Why don't you go catch up with your friends and have some fun?"

"That's okay, Connor," she said cheerfully. "I don't mind staying if you guys need some help."

"No, Connor's right, Luce," Jake said. "Thanks for taking those notes for us, but that's all we needed. You should go have some fun while you have the chance."

Lucinda smiled. "Okay, I'm off, then. See you guys around."

Connor watched her walk away, then turned back to Jake. "Look, I appreciate what you're saying, I really do, but there's no way Maggie will get to me like she did before. And I'm definitely not back together with her, if that's why you're so bent out of shape. This is just business."

"Business?" Jake said skeptically. "Didn't look like you were conducting business just now."

"I have to agree," Ian chimed in. "You two looked pretty friendly to me."

"Look, she's here with me because we made a deal. She's my date for the week and in exchange, I get her beer formulas."

Connor had informed his brothers last week that Maggie was the brains behind the Taylor James beers, so they knew how important those beer formulas were.

Jake pondered Connor's words for a moment. "Sounds like a pretty lopsided deal. What's she getting out of it?"

"The pleasure of my company."

Ian snorted. "Right. What's she really getting?"

"She needs to borrow some cash," Connor admitted.

"You're giving her money." Jake's eyes narrowed in on

him. "So basically, you're paying her to spend time with you. Do you know how sleazy that sounds?"

Connor rolled his eyes. "You're such a jerk. She needs the money for Angus."

"What?" Ian's eyes widened. "Why? Is he sick?"

"He's got something wrong with his heart."

"Damn it." Jake leaned his hip against the long conference table. "I hate to hear that."

Connor nodded. "Yeah, me, too. There's some new experimental drug that's perfect for him, but it's incredibly expensive and the insurance won't cover it."

"Then we should just give him the money," Ian said.

"Maggie's too proud to take the money without giving something in return. So she's giving up her recipes."

Jake was reluctantly impressed. "I guess that sounds reasonable."

"It is. So back off, because I've got this covered."

"Now you're scaring me again."

Connor ignored that. "And next time you see Maggie, be nice. Pretend Mom's watching."

"Aw, hell," Jake muttered.

"Yeah, and no more Vulcan death stare," Ian added, scowling at Jake. "You were even scaring *me* with that look."

Connor turned to leave. "I'll see you guys later. I've got to go find Maggie."

"Hey, wait," Jake said before Connor could get away. "Are you really sure she needs the money? I heard she was rolling in dough from her rich ex-husband."

"Where'd you hear that?"

"I don't know," he said, frowning as he tried to think about it. "One of her friends, I guess."

"What friends?" Ian scoffed. "I heard from Sarah Myers that all of Maggie's friends had turned on her."

"That's her own fault," Jake grumbled.

The fact was, Connor didn't really know much about what had happened, either, but that didn't mean he would put up with Jake's attitude. Connor smacked his brother's arm. "Whatever happened between Maggie and me is ancient history and none of your business, so stop being such a jerk about this."

"All right, all right," Jake said, holding his hands up. "I'll be nice."

"You bet your ass you will," Connor said ominously.

"But here's an idea," Jake said, his tone turning derisive. "Maybe you can fill us in on the *ancient history* one of these days." He used sarcastic air quotes for *ancient history,* as if he wasn't buying Connor's claim at all.

The sarcasm pissed Connor off to a whole new level and he made a move toward Jake. Ian quickly stepped between his two brothers, ever the peacemaker.

"Easy, there," Ian said, holding up his hands. "Both of you take a step back."

"Jackass," Connor muttered.

"Lamebrain," Jake countered.

"Don't sweat it, Connor," Ian said, then turned and gave Jake a fulminating glare. "We'll all behave ourselves like gentlemen."

"You're damn straight you will." Connor jabbed his finger at Jake. "And here's fair warning. I'm bringing Maggie to the Wellstone dinner tomorrow night, so you'd better treat her like a freaking goddess or you'll be watching the whole deal fall apart like a house of cards."

Connor decided to give Maggie some time to herself and, after wandering around the lobby for ten minutes, he stepped outside for some air. Crossing the terrace, he walked down to the boardwalk and headed south.

The sun was still bright, but the wind had come up and

turned blustery. Connor didn't mind the chill after so many hours spent inside the convention center.

He still wasn't sure why he had defended Maggie so stridently to his brothers, especially since most of what Jake had complained about was exactly how Connor had felt at one time. Didn't trust her, didn't understand her, didn't want to see her again.

But that was before Maggie had walked into his office a week ago. Since then, some of his opinions had shifted a little. And wasn't that perfectly natural? Especially after he'd found out that she hadn't exactly lived a charmed life all those years she'd been away. Still, he wasn't quite willing to cut her too much slack. At least, not until he found out exactly why she left him in the first place

He wouldn't mention it to his brothers, but he could admit to himself that he liked hanging out with her. Now and then, he caught glimpses of the old Maggie he'd known and loved, and okay, the fact that she was sexier than ever was a major point in her favor. So what was wrong with enjoying himself for a few days?

That didn't mean he trusted her, of course. There was no way she could ever restore the trust he'd once had in her. Nevertheless, when he heard his brothers talking smack about her, he didn't like it. Truth be told, their sniping had riled him up so much that he'd been tempted to punch out both of them. Not that Ian deserved it as much as Jake, but hey, Ian could always use a punch in the stomach, too, just on general principle.

The thought made him chuckle as he brushed his windblown hair back from his forehead. He loved his brothers, but sometimes they could be pains in the butt. Jake in particular had always been a hard-ass, especially when it came to trusting people. He was famous for saying that he hated liars, and once his trust was broken, he never looked back.

Connor didn't blame Jake for feeling that way. He knew

exactly where the distrust had come from. It was all thanks to their deceitful uncle Hugh and his damnable will. Hugh's relentless rivalry with their own father had extended beyond the grave, as the three brothers found out last year when it came time to read Uncle Hugh's last will and testament. A miserable man even on a good day, Hugh had attempted to pit Connor and his brothers against one another in an all-out fight for their inheritance.

So far, the brothers had outmaneuvered their uncle's Scottish lawyers and the ludicrous terms of the will. But all of that was irrelevant at the moment. Right now Connor just wanted Jake to lighten up around Maggie.

He did appreciate that Jake was worried about Maggie worming her way back into Connor's heart and maybe twisting it into a pretzel and leaving him for dead all over again. But Connor was a lot smarter and stronger now and he wasn't about to let that happen. So Jake had nothing to worry about on that front.

And besides, Connor reasoned, it wasn't as if Maggie had ever lied to Jake. Hell, Connor couldn't even swear that she'd ever lied to himself, either. She'd just left him. That was all. There had been no lies. No tears. No pretending. Maggie had simply walked out of his life one day and had never looked back.

Connor rubbed at a twinge in his chest and then swore crudely. This had to be heartburn or something. It couldn't possibly be the lingering memory of Maggie's desertion that was causing this stab of pain.

He sloughed off the ache and concentrated instead on the sight of a tarnished old fishing boat as it puttered into the harbor with its catch of the day. The crusty captain had a pipe shoved in his mouth and a bottle of beer in a handy cup holder next to the wheel.

Damn it. As much as it bugged Connor to admit it, Jake might have been right to question Connor's feelings for

Maggie. Especially since, like it or not, he still seemed to have a bit of a soft spot when it came to her. Which was a little ironic since he invariably turned hard as stone whenever she was around.

But that didn't mean he suddenly trusted her. He didn't, and wasn't sure he ever would again. And because of that, it wouldn't hurt to take a page out of Jake's book and be even more watchful around Maggie than he'd been before. That redheaded beauty was more than capable of slipping under his guard if he didn't remain on full alert from now on.

Connor walked back inside and immediately spotted her exiting an elevator and heading for the lobby. As he approached, she caught sight of him and stopped in her tracks.

"I was just going to go for a walk."

He took hold of her arm. "I just came in from a walk, but I'll go back out with you."

"That's not necessary."

"Yes, it is. You're my date, remember?"

"Oh, come on. You don't need me with you every minute of the day, do you?"

"Yes, I do." When her eyes widened, he quickly added, "Because we have a deal, in case you forgot."

"Right," she said, and sighed. "We have a deal. But that shouldn't mean I don't get a break once in a while. Especially after being the target of your brother's evil stink-eye stare."

He almost laughed but managed to check himself. He didn't blame her for ragging on Jake, but he wasn't about to tell her so. "I didn't notice."

"Oh, please! He was scowling at me the whole time I was standing there. He's about as subtle as a rhinoceros."

He shrugged. "Jake scowls so often I never think much about it. But admit it, it's not just my brothers that you have a problem with."

"What do you mean?"

"You think I didn't notice you racing in the opposite direction as soon as Sarah and her friends showed up? You left me to defend myself against them. That was cruel. They're your friends, not mine."

"They are not my friends," she said flatly, then began to chuckle. "And honestly? You're complaining about having three women drool all over you? Hang on to your every word? You didn't appear to be suffering, Connor."

He chuckled, then changed the subject. "Let's go upstairs and get jackets. It's chilly outside."

The elevator arrived and she stepped inside. Connor joined her and the elevator quickly filled up, so they kept their conversation mundane. A few minutes later, they stepped out on the twelfth floor and walked to the door of their suite.

As Connor keyed open the door, Maggie said, "I don't care what you had planned for dinner tonight. I'm going to the Crab Shack and I'm having a glass of wine."

Connor grinned. The Crab Shack was one of his favorite dive restaurants and it was only a half block away. "I'm up for that."

"You are?"

He opened the door for Maggie, then followed her inside. But before she could go any farther, he grabbed her arm. "Look, Maggie. I know Jake can be a jerk, but that's not really why you ran off, is it?"

"Of course not," Maggie said, not quite meeting his gaze. "I had things to do."

"Right."

"Fine." She draped her blazer on the back of the dining room chair. "Of course I ran off. Anyone would've if they'd seen the look he was giving me. If they'd felt the chill."

"The chill?"

"Yes, the deadly chill emanating from your brother that was aimed in my direction. Forget it." She shook her head in dismissal and walked into the bathroom to brush her hair. Connor followed her and leaned against the doorjamb to watch in the mirror while she brushed her hair.

"Okay," he conceded. "I might've noticed him staring at you, but he hasn't seen you in a long time. Maybe he was mesmerized by your beauty."

"You're funny."

"Not trying to be." Connor sat on the marble ledge next to the luxurious spa bathtub and made himself comfortable while she applied a fresh coat of lipstick. Her movements were so simple while being quite possibly the most sensual thing he'd seen in forever. It took every ounce of willpower he possessed to keep from grabbing hold of her and licking the color off her mouth, then covering every inch of her body in hot kisses.

Sadly, Maggie didn't look as though she'd be open to that plan at the moment, but he had all afternoon to convince her otherwise.

The thought had him growing hard again and he subtly adjusted himself while forcing himself to concentrate on business. "Here's the thing, Maggie. Tomorrow night, you and I and my brothers will be having dinner with some very important business associates. MacLaren Corporation is involved in a very sensitive and confidential transaction with this other group, and the last thing we need them to see is friction between you and Jake."

"If your meeting is so sensitive and confidential, why do you want me to be there? I know you don't trust me."

He stared at her for a long moment. She was stating exactly what he'd been thinking earlier, that he didn't trust her and never would. And yet…he did trust her. Maybe not as far as his heart was concerned, but this was different. "In this case, I do trust you. I know you wouldn't do anything to jeopardize our business."

She blinked in surprise. "Thank you. I appreciate that.

And you're right, I would never deliberately put your business at risk."

"So you'll play nicely with Jake."

"I'm happy to get along with everyone, Connor, but your problem lies with Jake. You need to talk to him." She waved a little wand thing as she spoke, then wiped the tip of it along her lips, causing them to grow even glossier and lusciously edible than before.

"I've...um." He gulped. It was getting more difficult to follow the conversation. "I've already given Jake an earful."

"Good, because the last thing I need in my life is more friction." She met his gaze in the mirror as understanding dawned. "So you *did* notice he was scowling at me."

"Of course I noticed. But like I said, that's his normal expression. I've learned to ignore it."

"It's pretty hard to ignore when you're the target."

Connor was forced to agree with her since he had also been the target of Jake's wrath within the past half hour. "I apologize for his idiocy. I hope you can overlook it and get along with him tomorrow night."

She zipped up her cosmetic bag and turned to gaze directly at him. "We'll be fine, Connor. I'm sure your brother wouldn't do anything to jeopardize an important business transaction."

"No, he wouldn't."

"And neither would I. So it's settled. Let's go to lunch."

"Wait." He gripped her shoulders lightly. "I want to make this official in case you didn't hear me a minute ago. I sincerely apologize for my brothers hurting your feelings. You didn't deserve it and it won't happen again. And if it does, one of them will have to die."

She beamed. "Thank you, Connor. I appreciate that." She was gazing up at him as if he were some kind of heroic Knight of the Round Table, which was so far from the truth it was laughable.

"I'm not sure you should thank me," he said. "I didn't punch his lights out or anything. I should've, but I didn't."

"Thank you anyway." She continued to stare at him, the soft trace of a smile on her lips, and he no longer had a choice. He kissed her.

He fought to take it slow and easy with her, even though he was consumed with a stark need for more. But the knowledge that Maggie might still be reeling from Jake's censure forced Connor to keep the contact light. And that was one more reason why he planned to knock his brother on his ass the next time he had the chance.

Knowing she hadn't expected his kiss and wasn't ready to take it further, Connor was nonetheless tempted to break down her barriers and fulfill his deepest need to take her. Right now. In every way possible. He wanted her clothes stripped off, her breasts in his hands, his mouth on her skin, her body slick with his sweat, her core filled with his shaft.

The image made his heart pound so hard and loud his eyes almost crossed.

Connor had never been the kind of man who required instant gratification. Stretching out the anticipation made the fulfillment of his goal so much sweeter, so much more worth the wait. But now the scent of her filled his head, intoxicating him, making it difficult to remember why he'd thought it better to wait. He burned for her, wanted her more than he'd ever wanted anything before. Now. He didn't want to wait another second.

He shifted and changed the angle of their kiss and covered her lips completely. She had the most incredibly sensual mouth he'd ever seen on a woman, and he couldn't get enough of it.

Ever since the night before when he'd been stupid enough to postpone their lovemaking, he'd been craving the touch of her lips again. Waiting and wondering when the right moment would come and he could take her in his arms and fulfill his most ardent fantasies.

A soft sigh fluttered in her throat, and Connor took it as a sign of her desire for more. He eased her lips apart with his tongue and plunged inside her warmth, where her tongue tangled with his in a pleasurable whirl of desire.

As they kissed, a distant part of Connor's mind flashed to the past when he and Maggie had been joined at the lip. They'd shared hundreds, maybe thousands of kisses back then, so why did her kiss today feel so completely different and brand-new? As though they'd never kissed before this moment.

They weren't the same people, he thought. They were older, definitely. Smarter, too, he hoped. Back then, Connor had worshiped the ground Maggie walked upon. He'd treated her like spun silk, a rare treasure, something to be cherished above all else. Maybe that was why she'd left him. Maybe he'd been too wrapped up in her to notice she wasn't happy. He still didn't know.

But the Maggie in his arms today was a flesh-and-blood woman. Complicated. Beautiful. Normal. He no longer had any expectations that she was anything other than that. And that made everything different.

Better, he thought again.

When she moaned, he ended the kiss and gazed at her. "In case you couldn't guess, I want you, Maggie."

She studied him for a long moment; then she sighed. "Does this mean I'm going to miss my dinner?"

He laughed and ran his hands up and down her arms. "Only if you say so. It might kill me, but I'm following your lead—for right now."

Tonight, though, he would be the one in charge. And there was no doubt in his mind as to how they would be spending the evening.

"So, what do you want, Maggie?"

"I want… I…" She closed her eyes and leaned her forehead against his chest.

"You want…" he prompted, using his finger to lift her chin so he could meet her gaze.

"Damn it, Connor, just kiss me again."

His smile grew and he pulled her closer. "Be happy to oblige."

His mouth took hers in a white-hot kiss and Maggie met him with the same level of passion, mixed with a new level of confidence and enthusiasm. It seemed to Connor that now that she'd made the choice, Maggie could relax and go with her instincts. Maybe it came from being the one to make the decision, or maybe she just needed to hear him say how much he wanted her. Not that she couldn't have figured it out on her own by looking at a strategic part of his anatomy, but it probably also helped that he'd voiced how ridiculously desperate he was to taste her and touch her.

He refused to question her change of heart. He was just pitifully grateful that she wanted the same thing he did.

She parted her lips to allow him entrance and met each stroke of his tongue with her own. As his hands swept over her back and dipped down to lightly grasp her gorgeous butt, she let out another soft groan and arched into him.

Connor gave a mental shout-out to whatever gods were in charge of the really important things—like Maggie's body. Her well-sculpted arms. The smooth line of her stomach. The shapely curve of her thighs. Not to mention her delectable mouth. She was temptation personified and he couldn't resist any part of her. Never could.

That was probably why it had taken him so long to get her out of his system. But he *had* gotten over her.

This time, things would be different, he thought, as he slid his hand up and cupped her breast.

This time it was all about physical pleasure, pure and

simple. No hearts, no emotions, no pain. No more thinking about the past. From here on, there was only pleasure.

"Connor, I want…"

"So do I, baby," he whispered, and swooped her up into his arms.

"Oh, you never did that before," she blurted, then laughed playfully and wrapped her arms around his neck.

"I must've been crazy," he muttered, and carried her into the bedroom, were he laid her down gently on the comforter.

He followed her down and pulled her into his arms, where they gave and took in equal measure as they rolled together, exploring, begging, melting into each other as they each demanded more and more.

Connor moved up onto his knees and straddled her thighs. "You're wearing too many clothes," he said, sliding his hands under her top. "I do like this sweater."

She smiled dreamily. "Thank you."

In a blur, he whipped it up and over her head and tossed it aside.

She laughed in surprise, then sighed as he ran his hands along her bare shoulders, down her sides and across her stomach.

"I like this better," he said.

"Me, too."

He cupped her breasts and leaned over to kiss the soft roundness. Swiftly unhooking her bra, he tossed it, as well. "Better and better."

"Connor," she whispered, and moaned when he used his thumbs to tease her nipples to peak. He moved in with his mouth, taking first one breast, then the other, sucking and licking, nibbling and tasting until she was writhing under him.

He moved lower, kissing her stomach and nuzzling her belly button as he slid lower still. He slowly unzipped her pants, planting more kisses as he exposed more skin. Pulling them off, he rose to gaze at her body. "God, you're beautiful."

"Connor," she said on a sigh.

"I'm right here." He gazed at her, saw that her eyes were bright with desire. Her thick red hair was spread out in waves across the pillow like an aura. Her lips were plump and wet from the touch of his own. All she wore now was a pair of skimpy pink lace panties, the stuff of male dreams. He slid two fingers under the edge to tease her, but only succeeded in straining his already shaky control. His body was hard and aching and he couldn't wait another minute to do the one and only thing he wanted to do. Bury himself inside her.

He jumped off the bed and undressed in a heartbeat, then found one of the many condoms he'd been smart enough to pack. He quickly tore it open and sheathed himself, then returned to the bed, where she was watching him with a hunger that matched his own.

"All dressed up and ready to go?" she said saucily.

"That's right." He slid closer and planted a kiss on her smooth shoulder. "Now, where was I? Let's see."

He moved lower again, kissing and licking his way down her body. He stopped to taste her breasts once again, filling his senses, then moving along the soft contours of her stomach and hips. She was breathless by the time he reached the apex of her sleek thighs.

"Ah yes," he murmured as he reached beneath her panties with his fingers to find her hot, moist core. "I was right here."

She trembled and moaned her need as his fingers began

to stroke her inner heat, taking her to the edge and back again, driving her to the brink of release, then pulling her back once more. Her soft pleas became groans of need and Connor was certain he'd never known such all-consuming desire before. Not even ten years ago when all he'd wanted was Maggie. This was more. This was bigger. He craved her with every fiber of his being.

He hooked his thumbs around the band of her panties and tugged them off slowly, killing himself with pleasure as he watched them slide over her curvy hips and down her shapely legs. When he reached her ankles, she nudged him away with one foot while she used the other to fling the panties across the room.

He laughed and glanced up at her. Her full lips were curved in a sexy smile and her brandy-hued eyes gleamed with feminine power and pleasure. She'd never looked more beautiful to him and he decided, in that moment, that he needed honesty between them.

"I've wanted you in my bed since I saw you last week," he said, moving closer and positioning himself. In one swift motion, he entered her and crushed his mouth against hers. She gripped his shoulders as their bodies rocked together in a sensual, synchronous rhythm that seemed to arise from within them and overtake them effortlessly.

He felt her heart beating in time to his, kissed the smooth surface of her neck and shoulders. He'd never felt more alive as he strained to bring her the ultimate pleasure possible while holding out on the same for himself for as long as humanly possible. But as her body strained against his, as her sumptuous breasts pressed into his chest, as her stunning legs wrapped more tightly around his waist, he felt a stab of need stronger than any he'd experienced before. He pressed more deeply, filling her completely, building up the hunger within them both until they were clinging to the edge of sheer passion.

She fell first, crying out his name and shuddering in his arms, leaving Connor overwhelmed by a bone-deep sense of fulfillment. With one last driving thrust, he echoed her cry with his own and a dark, wild rapture hurtled him over the edge.

Seven

What did you do?

She'd had sex with Connor, she reminded herself, with a mental cuff to the head. Wasn't it obvious? The man himself was still warm, sexy, naked and snuggled beside her in their big comfy bed.

Sex with Connor. It had been even better than she remembered. More than wonderful, it was spectacular. Better than fireworks. Or rainbows. It was awesome. The best sex she'd experienced in…forever? Hard to believe, but Connor was a better lover than he used to be, and he'd been pretty darned good back in the day.

Connor had always been wonderful, thoughtful and giving. But now he was so much more than that. He was powerful and agile and…oh, mercy. Did she already mention *awesome?*

But that wasn't the point, was it? The point was, she had done something horribly wrong and stupid. How many times had she reminded herself in the past week that Connor MacLaren was out for revenge, pure and simple? How many ways had she practiced saying *No!* to him?

And with one kiss, her stratagem had crumbled. Granted, it had been a very, very *good* kiss, but now what? She'd let go of every last qualm she'd brandished as a first line of defense and now she was left with, well, nothing. If she were smart, she would get dressed and go back home to her grandfather and the goats.

More than anything else, this proved what a hypocrite

she was. After all, she'd spent years trying to avoid risks, ridding her life of any little thing that might bring her pain, and here she was again, risking it all for a chance to…to what? Find a love to last a lifetime? Yeah, right. With the guy everyone—including him—thought she'd unceremoniously dumped ten years ago? Get real.

Maggie squeezed her eyes shut even tighter.

She wished she could blame Connor for coercing her, but he'd made a point of insisting that it was her decision to continue. Awfully clever of him.

Well, Maggie would just have to chalk this up as one more bad decision in a lifetime full of them.

Alan would say—

Stop!

Maggie cringed. She had a long-standing rule never to start a sentence with her ex-husband's name.

Connor stretched, then turned and leaned up on his elbow to gaze down at her. "You're thinking too much. I can hear your brain ticking away."

"Sorry. Sometimes my inner thoughts can get pretty loud."

Smiling, he brushed a strand of hair off her forehead, then slowly sobered. That couldn't be a good sign. "Maggie, that was…"

A mistake?

A horrible error in judgment?

Was he waiting for her to finish the sentence? Was there a multiple-choice response?

"Phenomenal," he murmured, and bent his head to kiss the tender skin beneath her chin. "Incredible. Mind-bending."

"Awesome?" she suggested lightly.

"Beyond awesome." He nudged the blanket down so he could kiss and nibble her neck and her ear and her jaw and, oh, sweet mother, Maggie's synapses were starting to sizzle. She wanted him all over again.

Phenomenal, he'd said. Would this be a good time to jump up and do a little happy dance? Maybe not. And really, even though the sex was good—or rather, damn good, phenomenal, awesome—it didn't change the bigger picture, the one in which Maggie knew she'd screwed up royally. So right now she needed to stop fooling around and think about her next move. She should leave. But what if he changed his mind about their deal? What if he changed the terms? Was it awful of her to wonder about that at a time like this? Yes, but...oh dear, should she pack her bags? Should she eat something first? She ought to think about—

"You are so beautiful, Maggie," he said, trailing kisses along her breastbone. Then he reached for her. "Come here."

She stared at his tousled dark hair, ran her hands along the strong muscles of his shoulders and back and pondered whether she was making another mistake again. Oh, hell, was there any doubt?

He lifted his head and met her gaze. "Trust me, Maggie?"

Biting her lip, she stared into his dark eyes and wondered if she'd ever had a choice. He smiled then, and so did she. Because of course, she'd always had a choice.

"Yes," Maggie whispered, and didn't have to think anymore.

As the sun was setting over the ocean, Maggie and Connor slipped on jeans, sweatshirts and sneakers and walked down the boardwalk to the Crab Shack.

With peanut shells on the floor and a monstrous grinning crab crawling on the roof, it shouldn't have been romantic, but Maggie loved it. They grabbed an empty table next to the full-length plate-glass window and ordered wine. The last arc of the sun shot coral and pink cloud trails across the sky until the sun finally sank beneath the horizon. Once it was gone completely, streetlamps began to twinkle to life along the boardwalk. Their server brought their wine along with a votive candle to shed some light on the menus.

"I don't suppose you want lobster," Connor asked after a minute of perusing the specials.

"I love lobster. I haven't had it in years." She closed her menu and took a sip of wine. "Yes, that's what I'm having."

"I figured you might've gotten tired of it after all that time you spent in Boston."

"Oh no, no," she said, chuckling. "Lobster was not allowed."

"Allowed?" He frowned at her. "Is this about your ex? Because I've got to tell you, Maggie, the guy sounds like a real jackass."

She smiled. "What a lovely description. It suits him perfectly."

Their waiter was back with bread and butter and took their orders.

After the waiter walked away, Connor leaned forward. "I've got to ask you something. If the guy was such an ass, why did you ever…" He flopped back in his chair and held up his hand to her. "Wait. Never mind. Don't answer that."

"No, it's okay," she said, sighing as she buttered a slice of sourdough bread. "Go ahead and ask whatever it is you're wondering about. You deserve answers."

He pulled off a hunk of bread and popped a small chunk of it into his mouth. Did he really want to hear all the reasons why she'd stopped loving him? Hell, no. But she was right. After all this time, not to mention the past four hours they'd spent in bed together, it would be smart to get some answers. "Okay, I'll ask. Why'd you leave me for him?"

She stopped chewing abruptly and tilted her head in confusion. "Connor, I didn't leave you for him. You and I had already broken up a month earlier."

He was taken aback. "No, we didn't."

"Yes, we did," she said softly. "We broke up the day you announced that you and your brothers were going to spend a week at some skydiving camp."

He wanted to ask her what alternative universe she was living in, but he kept it civil. "Maggie, that's just not true."

"Yes, it is. I remember it as if it were yesterday because I was devastated." She tapped her fingers nervously against the base of her wineglass. "I was so proud of myself because I'd managed to keep breathing when you went on that white-water rafting trip to the most dangerous river in the country. But then you went off with your brothers to climb El Capitan in Yosemite and I was breathing into a paper bag the whole time. When you told me about the skydiving, it was the last straw for me. I told you that if you went away, I wouldn't be here for you when you got back." She waved her hand in disgust. "Such a stupid, girlish threat, but I meant it at the time."

He frowned, remembering her words in that last conversation, but not realizing their full implication at the time.

She continued. "So after I said that, you said, 'That's too bad, babe. I guess we both have things we've gotta do.' And that was it. We said goodbye and you hung up the phone. Believe me, Connor. I remember that conversation. I remember staring at the phone and then bursting into tears. My mother probably remembers, too. I drove her crazy that summer."

Apparently everyone had grasped her meaning but him. "I thought you were telling me that you were going away for a while, like, on vacation. I figured, I'd be gone a week, come home and then you'd be gone a few weeks. So we'd miss each other's company for maybe a month, but we'd get back together at the end of summer."

Her face had turned pale. "No. I meant that I wouldn't be with you anymore."

He felt his chest constrict as he considered her words. "So you were already over me."

"Oh no! No, I loved you so much, but you scared me to death. Connor, don't you remember how I used to tell you that you deserved a woman who enjoyed taking risks? Someone just like you?"

He swirled his wineglass absently. "Yeah, you said it a lot. I thought it was a little joke, because I always thought we were perfect together."

Her eyes glittered with tears as she shook her head. "No, it wasn't a joke. I wish it was, but I couldn't stand it when you took chances with your life."

"My life?"

"You and your brothers were always going off to hike up some sheer cliff, or ski over some avalanche, or ride horses down a treacherous canyon path."

He gave a lopsided grin. "The Grand Canyon trip. Hell, Maggie, we used to do that kind of stuff all the time. Not so much anymore. But I don't see why it was such a big deal to you."

"Believe me, it was a big deal. I would sit at home holding my breath, waiting for the phone call from the morgue."

And that's when Connor suddenly remembered that Maggie's father had died in a hiking accident in Alaska. He'd always known about it, but had never connected the dots. Damn, no wonder all of his wild sporting activities used to freak her out. He sat back in the chair feeling wretched, his appetite gone. "I'm so sorry, Maggie."

"So am I." She smiled sadly. "When you said you were going skydiving for a week? Oh, my God, I almost fainted. I couldn't take it anymore. Most of my life, I've been afraid to take those kinds of risks. I was ultracautious, don't you remember? I didn't even try out for cheerleading because I thought I might get hurt. It was all because of the way my dad died. He was just like you and your brothers, always looking for the next big adrenaline rush. His death was so devastating to me and my mom, there was no way I was going to put myself through that kind of pain again with you."

"Damn, Maggie." He realized now that he must've scared the hell out of her on a daily basis. As the youngest brother, he'd always been the one to take on any stupid challenge or death-defying dare. He really was lucky to be alive. "I guess that was the last straw you were talking about."

"It was." She reached across the table for his hand. "I'm sorry I didn't explain things more clearly, but I guess at the time, I just panicked."

"I'm sorry, too." He squeezed her hand in his. "If we'd taken the time to talk it out, we might've…well, who knows what could've happened?"

She gazed at him and her smile faded. "It seemed too selfish to ask you to change your lifestyle for me."

He shook his head and stared out at the darkening vista. The ocean was rougher now and the choppy whitecaps gleamed like shards of ice in the reflected light. "I would've done anything for you, Maggie."

"I know," she whispered, and blinked away tears. "But it wouldn't have been fair."

The waiter arrived with two huge platters, each with a full-size lobster, drawn butter and baked potatoes with everything on them. He poured more wine for each of them, wished them *bon appétit* and left them alone.

Connor chuckled somberly. "Are you even hungry after all this depressing talk?"

Maggie sniffled as she looked down at her lobster and then over at him. "You bet I am."

He laughed. "That's my girl." And they both started eating, their appetites and humor instantly restored.

They spent the next few minutes in silence as they wolfed down the perfectly prepared food. Finally Connor took a break and sat back in his chair. He reached for his wine and took a sip, then said, "Mind if I ask you something that might put me in a happier mood?"

"But not me?" She laughed shortly. "Sure, go ahead."

"Why'd you marry this joker?" Then, even though he knew the answer, he asked, "And what's his name again? Albert? Arthur?"

"It's Alan. Alan Cosgrove, and that's the last time I'll use his actual name out loud. I'm afraid of summoning the devil."

He chuckled. "Like *Beetlejuice?*"

"Exactly!"

It had been one of their all-time favorite movies back in the day.

Maggie drank down a hearty gulp of wine and seemed to brace herself before answering. It was one more way Connor could tell that the guy had been a real piece of work.

"After you and I broke up," she began, "I cried myself silly for weeks."

"Good to hear."

She laughed. "My mother finally sent me off to visit my cousin Jane in Boston. Jane had a summer day job, so I spent my mornings wallowing in grief and my afternoons walking for miles around Boston. There were so many charming neighborhoods and I think I saw them all. One day I walked into a fancy art gallery in the Back Bay and that's where I met him."

"Ashcroft," he said helpfully.

"Yes." She giggled. "*Ashcroft* was wealthy, nice looking, seemed stable enough. He enjoyed quiet walks, art galleries and foreign films."

"Much like myself."

She gave a ladylike snort. "Right." She went on to explain that the guy she met had seemed safe and sane and unlikely to do anything that would worry her excessively.

"Unlike myself."

"Sadly," she murmured. "At the time, I thought it was important that he wasn't a risk taker. I was so stupid."

"We were both young," he said, giving her a break.

"I suppose," Maggie continued, "but despite how good Ashcroft might've looked on paper, in reality, he was a jerk and probably a sociopath."

There was no *probably* about it, Connor thought, but didn't say it aloud.

"It turned out that he was being forced into marriage by his iron-fisted mother, who had decreed that it was time for him to find a wife. Sybil—that's his mother's name," Maggie explained. "Sybil had suggested that he find someone pretty enough, who was malleable, penniless and had very few ties to Boston. It would be easier to control her that way, she said."

"Let me get this straight. His *mother* was telling him this?"

Maggie nodded. "Yes. She definitely knew her boy."

"This is creeping me out," Connor said. "But don't stop. I want to hear it all."

She grinned. "I'm not sure I can stop now that I'm on a roll." She took a quick bite of her baked potato, then continued. "A month after we were married, Sybil called me into her sitting room to let me know how well I'd met the criteria to be her daughter-in-law. Then she proceeded to tell me everything that was wrong with me."

"She doesn't exactly sound like Mom-of-the-Year."

"She was peachy," Maggie said, and shivered. "But the good news was that I had also fulfilled Ashcroft's requirements for a suitable wife."

"Can't wait to hear his list." He held up his hand. "He obviously wanted someone beautiful, right?"

"Thank you," she said with a grateful smile. "But you really need to hear the prerequisites he gave his mother."

"Oh, I get it," Connor said. "She was the one who was going to find him a wife."

"That was the plan."

"But then he met you."

"Yes, but I had to pass muster with his mother first."

Connor shook his head. "What a guy."

"You have no idea," she murmured, her lips curving into a frown.

Connor didn't want her going too far down memory lane over this jerk, so he shot her a quick grin. "Come on, let's hear it. What did Weird Al want in a wife?"

She chuckled. "That's a perfect nickname for him. Okay, he specifically wanted someone who wasn't fat, didn't speak with a pronounced drawl, didn't snore and didn't chew with her mouth open."

Connor stared at her for a few long seconds. "Come on. You're kidding."

"If only," she said, smothering a laugh. "Sybil told me that Ashcroft was very sensitive about bodily sounds and emissions."

Connor snorted. "Yeah, most obsessive-compulsive anal-retentive types tend to be that way."

"If only I'd known this before the wedding," Maggie said. "But Ashcroft knew how to put on a good act. He swept me off my feet, promised me the moon and convinced me to marry him. What an idiot I was."

Connor didn't respond to that one, since he wholeheartedly agreed. "So, once you were married, what happened?"

"If you want to hear the gory details, I'm going to need more wine first," she said, grinning ruefully.

Connor chuckled and reached for the wine bottle. "Yeah, I think I might need a little more, too."

"Okay, the day we got married, we moved into his mother's mansion in Boston's Beacon Hill."

"You lived with his mom the whole time?"

"Yeah," she said. "They were close."

Connor almost spit his wine out. "They were demented."

"That, too." She speared a chunk of lobster and popped it into her mouth. "Oh, and none of my family were invited to the wedding, did I mention that? And within a few days of the ceremony, he was insisting that I cut off all ties with them."

"The better to isolate and control you."

"Yeah." She gazed at Connor. "I wasn't really smart about any of this. I think I was still traumatized about breaking up with you and I just kind of went along with things. It wasn't easy, because his mother was really cold and unbending. And he got worse as time went on. I just couldn't do anything to please either one of them."

"I wish you'd called me."

"I do, too, Connor." She reached across the table and touched his hand. "But I was adrift. After our last conversation, I didn't think you were all that interested in hearing from me. I wasn't sure of myself anymore. They did a good job of whittling away at my confidence."

"They sound like experts."

"Oh, they were." Her eyes hazed a bit as she remembered more. "After seven long years, I finally grew some gumption and decided it was time to divorce them both. And the very day I made an appointment to see a lawyer, Sybil died of a massive heart attack."

"Whoa."

"She left all her money to Ashcroft. And on the day of her funeral, he informed me that he was divorcing *me*."

Connor let out a string of expletives. "He did you a favor. You know that, right?"

"Oh, I know it," she said fiercely. "But even on the occasion of his mother's death, he couldn't leave it alone. No, he had to go on and on, explaining how unsuitable I was for him. How I had been nothing more than a convenience to him."

"He should be glad he's still breathing," he muttered.

"A *convenience*," Maggie repeated slowly, her hands tightening into fists. "That son of a bitch."

"Literally," Connor muttered.

She waved her anger away. "The divorce was a gift, frankly, because it meant I was blessedly free of him. He tried so hard to break my spirit, but he never broke my heart, thank God. And I'm so glad he saved me the trouble of trying to divorce him."

"Because he would've fought you to the bitter end."

"That's right." She chuckled. "Irony was always lost on Ashcroft."

"No sense of humor, that guy."

She laughed. "So I took my miniscule divorce settlement, swallowed my pride and came back home to Point Cairn. And here we are."

But Connor knew that wasn't the end of the story. His eyes narrowed on her. "Did he hurt you?"

"Physically?" She hesitated. "Not really." Then she added, "To be honest, he didn't care much for anything physical. He preferred to demoralize me mentally and emotionally."

Connor leaned forward. "We can change the subject, Maggie."

"No," she insisted, waving her fork back and forth. "I want to talk about it, because I never got to. Except to a therapist and that wasn't very satisfying. I thought when I came home, I would have my old girlfriends around to help me hash things out and get rid of those old feelings. But the girls weren't exactly happy to see me show up again."

Understanding dawned. In the years after Maggie left town, all of their friends had rallied around him and turned Maggie into the bad guy. Connor had never tried to change their opinions of Maggie because that's what he had thought, too. "That's why you ran in the other direction when you saw Sarah and the others."

She smiled tightly. "Pretty much."

"Jeez, Maggie, you've had a rough time of it."

"Oh, please, it's nothing I can't handle." She airily brushed away his concern but then began to laugh at herself. "Okay, yeah. It was really bad there for a while. Grandpa's goats became my best friends."

Connor chuckled as he poured the last of the wine into their glasses. "So you didn't have your girlfriends to hash things out with, but you've got me. I'm here. I'll help you get through it all. Tell me everything you went through with this clown Ashcroft."

She beamed a hopeful smile at him. "Really?"

"Come on." He gestured with his hand. "Come on, tell me the rest of it."

"Where shall I start?" She inhaled deeply, then said in a rush, "Okay. Well, he bought all my clothes for me."

"Hmm." Connor frowned. "I guess that's…nice?"

Her lips twisted sardonically. "Believe me, he didn't do it to be nice."

"Oh, right. That jerk." He took a sip of wine before advancing on the topic. "So…what kind of stuff did he make you wear?"

She laughed. "Probably not what you're thinking. No spandex or anything. He wanted me to be seen in expensive classics, knits and wools, sweater sets, a lot of plaids, skirts, shirtdresses, sensible shoes, pearls. Nothing garish or low class, like blue jeans or boots."

"Idiot."

"Thank you! You make a really good girlfriend."

They both laughed, and then Connor said, "Did you work during your marriage?" He struggled to get that last word out.

"Work?" Her laugh was a soft trill. "No. I couldn't work."

He nodded. "No jobs available?"

"Oh, I suppose there were jobs, but I had no skills."

He frowned. "Yes, you do."

She stared out the window for a moment, then gazed over at Connor. "But even if I could get a job, how would I get from my house to my workplace?"

"By car?"

"Oh no. I couldn't have a car because I might get lost or crash it."

"He told you that?" He squinted at her, puzzled. "But you were always a good driver."

"I know," she said with a sigh, and dunked a small piece of lobster in warm butter.

Connor took one last bite of his baked potato and it tasted like sand. He couldn't even imagine how his Maggie had lived through all this degradation and come out so healthy and normal. And what kind of vicious creep was Ashcroft to have a great girl like Maggie and treat her so badly?

"On the other hand," Connor hedged, "he had money, so you probably didn't need to work."

"True, I didn't need any extra money," she said breezily. "I would've just squandered it on frivolous things."

He studied her as he sipped his wine. "You never seemed like a frivolous person to me."

"I'm not. But he didn't agree. He thought I needed more discipline. His mother agreed with him that I was helpless in so many ways. Once we were married, he began to criticize minor things. Just here and there, you know? But after a few years, he was taking daily jabs at my appearance, my weight, my personality, my lack of social skills. You name it."

"God, what an idiot," he muttered, shaking his head in bemusement.

"That's putting it nicely. And as bad as he was, his mother could be downright evil sometimes."

"I wish I'd known. I would've rescued you."

"My hero."

The waiter placed a basket of fresh bread and butter on the table. Connor held the basket out for her, then took a piece of bread for himself. He took a bite, then waved at her to continue. "Come on, girlfriend, tell me more. Get it all out."

Maggie chuckled. "You're enjoying this too much."

"Believe me, I'm not." In fact, he was imagining finding this guy just to plant a fist in his arrogant face. "But it seems like the more you talk about how awful they were, the more relaxed you get. And I like to see that. So, anything else you want to tell me?"

"I'm afraid if I get started, I won't be able to stop." She took a quick sip of her wine. "I think what I hated most was that my opinions never mattered. They considered me either too naive or just plain stupid, depending on the situation. He always liked to tell me how sad it was that I was so intellectually challenged."

"That's it." Connor shoved his chair back from the table. He was only half kidding when he muttered, "I'm really going to kill him."

She laughed and clapped her hands. "Thank you. You're officially my best friend."

"Yeah, I am," he said, easing back into his chair, though it cost him to give her a smile. "And don't forget it."

The following afternoon, Connor stared out the bay window of the Marin Club, taking in the view of clear blue skies and tumultuous waves crashing against the sandy shore. Though he was here to meet with his brothers, all he could think about was Maggie, and not just because of the incredible sex they'd had that morning. No, she was on his mind because he couldn't forget the horror story she'd related at dinner the night before. He just wished he'd had an inkling of what she'd been going through. Damn it, he'd been so clueless back then he hadn't even realized they'd broken up. If he'd known how Maggie really felt, he would have canceled that stupid skydiving trip in a heartbeat. And he might have prevented her from running off and falling into the trap of that creep husband and his twisted mother. One phone call from Maggie and Connor would've jumped on a plane and rescued her from that hell house she'd been living in.

His thoughts were interrupted when the waitress came over and took their drink orders. Jake had called this impromptu meeting with his brothers to talk over some important family business. They'd decided to meet here instead of the festival hotel in order to avoid any big ears that might be tempted to listen in on their conversation.

The Marin Club wasn't actually a club at all, but a bar and grill the brothers had been coming to for years. The service was good, the drinks were cold and the food was great.

The waitress set their drinks on the table. "Here you go, boys. Scotch for you, Ian. Pint of IPA for Connor and your martini, Jake. Extra dry, lemon twist."

"Perfect," Connor said, taking the pint glass from her.

"You boys are so dressed up in your suits and ties this afternoon. Is there some big party I should know about?"

Jake grinned. "We've got a business dinner to go to after this."

"Ah," she said. "Not quite as exciting as I imagined, but I hope you have fun."

"Thanks, Sherry," Jake said. "You're the best."

She winked at him, slid the black plastic bill case onto the table and strolled away humming. She was an old friend of their mother's and could always count on the MacLaren boys for a large tip.

"Cheers," Ian said, holding up his glass. They all clinked their drinks together, then sipped.

"Okay, what's up?" Connor said after taking a satisfying taste of his drink, a well-crafted English pale ale that he'd been ordering for years.

Jake gave each of them his patented scowl. "I heard from the Scottish lawyers again."

"What's their problem?" Connor asked. "We've still got a few months before the terms of the will have to be met."

"They're getting antsy."

"No, they're getting pushy," Connor said.

"What do you expect?" Ian said. "They're lawyers."

"Yeah," Connor agreed. "But they're just going to have to wait until one of us can take some time off."

"It's not that I care what they think," Jake said, "but I do believe we're reaching the point where one of us will have to fly over there and survey the property, just to see what's involved."

"It's basically some land and a big old house," Ian said, shrugging. "We've all done real estate deals. What's the big mystery?"

Jake stared into his cocktail and frowned. "The lawyer mentioned something about crofters."

"We've got crofters?" Connor said.

Ian looked puzzled. "You mean, like squatters?"

"No," Jake said. "These are tenants who live and work the land around the castle. We pay them."

"We do?"

"Yeah, so whoever buys the land has to buy the crofters, too. They're a package deal."

Disgruntled, Ian said, "What if we don't want crofters? And it's kind of weird to be selling people, don't you think?"

"I doubt we're actually selling the people," Connor said dryly.

Jake shook his head in frustration. "This is why somebody has to go over there."

"One of you should go," Connor said immediately.

"Why not you?" Ian said.

"Because I've got boots-on-the-ground responsibilities up here. I've got twenty-seven new products ready to hit the market, we have three new farmers who want to join the artisanal league and we're training a replacement manager at the brewpub."

Ian looked askance. "Oh, so you're saying our meager office jobs are expendable, is that it?"

Connor grinned back at him. It was a long-standing rivalry among the brothers, with each of them claiming to work harder than the others. But in Connor's case, it was true. Maybe he didn't handle the corporate stuff, like finances or marketing or hiring, thank God. But he did have sole responsibility for the day-to-day production of eight different facilities, including the brewery itself and the brewpub in town, both of which had put their company on the map in the first place.

"You're the natural choice to go," Connor said to Ian. "You could check things out with the castle, then take a detour south and visit Gordon. Make sure he's still willing to grow our hops."

Ian flashed Connor a dirty look. "Everything's fine with the damn hops. The next batch will arrive on time, right after the drying season. So back off."

"Touchy," Connor muttered, exchanging glances with Jake. It always irritated Ian when they brought up the subject of his recent breakup with his gorgeous wife, Samantha. Her eccentric father, Gordon McGregor, lived in an ashram west of Kilmarnock where he grew the hops and many of the bitter herbs used exclusively in MacLaren beers. The trade winds that warmed the west coast of Scotland provided the perfect climate for Gordon's hops and they were among the finest the MacLarens had ever used for their beers. While Connor cared very much for his sister-in-law Sam and was sorry she and Ian had split, he knew that if they lost their main source for those rare Scottish hops, it could be disastrous.

"I can't go right now, either," Jake realized.

Ian rolled his eyes. "Why not?"

"I'm in the middle of planning the senior staff retreat," he explained. "I won't be able to go for at least three months."

"Look, we don't have to make up excuses for the lawyers," Ian reasoned. "As soon as one of us gets a break, whoever it is will go to Scotland, meet with the lawyers, check out the castle and list it for sale."

"Sounds good to me," Connor said. "I can't wait to get rid of it."

"And Uncle Hugh's bad juju along with it," Jake muttered.

Ian nodded. "Mom will be glad, too."

"She's been wanting the whole problem to disappear from day one."

"Yeah," Jake said. "Uncle Hugh pretty much ruined her life."

"But she rallied just fine," Connor said with a hint of pride. "She made a good life for all of us once she got over here."

At that, the three men spontaneously clinked their glasses together and drank in silence.

Despite acquiring the castle and all the land for miles around it after their father died, Uncle Hugh continued to be a bitter man to the very end. Since he'd never had children and hated his own brother, he fashioned his last will and testament to deliberately create an irreparable rift among his nephews, forcing them to compete against each other for their inheritance.

His will provided that all the MacLaren money, land

and power would go to whichever brother had acquired the most wealth by the twenty-fifth anniversary of their father's death. As the date grew closer, Jake was contacted by the Scottish lawyers, who required the brothers to send financial reports in order to determine which of them would eventually inherit.

That final date was coming up fast.

Connor, Ian and Jake had no intention of complying with their uncle's wishes. They had vowed at a young age not to fight against each other for the sake of a plot of land and a big old house, especially if it fulfilled their horrible uncle's wishes. Frankly, none of them could even picture the castle in their minds since Uncle Hugh had taken possession of it when they were all too young to remember it. Their mother called it "a cold, crumbling pile of Scottish stone" and cursed it on a daily basis.

The plain fact was, their home was Northern California now. They didn't want the castle or the land. So no matter which brother "won" Uncle Hugh's blood money, the three of them planned to sell the Scottish land and the castle and split the proceeds three ways.

Jake savored his cocktail. "I'll call the lawyers back and let them know that one of us will get over there within the next three months."

"Sounds good," Ian said, and glanced at his wristwatch. "So, everyone ready for this dinner with the Wellstones?"

"Yeah," Jake said, reaching for his wallet. "I'll be meeting my date at the restaurant a few minutes ahead of time."

"Sounds good." Connor stood and tossed a ten-dollar bill on the table. "I've got to get back and pick up Maggie. I'll see you guys there."

Maggie paced back and forth in front of the living room window of the suite, occasionally glancing up to check the time. Connor would arrive any minute now to take her to the important dinner with Mr. Wellstone and his sons. They planned to close a major deal tonight, and Maggie had to be on her best behavior.

So it might not be appropriate to stumble and fall on her butt.

That's why she was walking around, trying to get used to high heels again. It had been three long years since she'd been forced to wear anything like these killer stilettos. Not since the days when Alan—er, Ashcroft—required her to dress up for the fancy society balls and dinner parties they were constantly attending.

Along with her ex-husband and his crabby mother, Maggie didn't miss high heels at all.

The dress she wore was one of the few she'd salvaged from her marriage, a little black dress, short and beautifully beaded around the edges, with flattering cap sleeves and a sweetheart neckline that showed the barest hint of cleavage. She didn't mind wearing it now because Ashcroft and his mother had hated it.

Maggie was surprised at how much relief she felt after talking to Connor about her crazy marriage. There had been a few moments at dinner last night when she'd almost burst into tears, but it hadn't been because of the bad memories. It had been because Connor was so sweet to listen, so quick to take her side, so heroic in his defense of her. And the amazing sex afterward had helped, too.

One thing Connor had never asked, though, was why she'd stayed with the man for so many years. Why didn't she leave Ashcroft in the very beginning when he first started picking on her?

Maggie was so glad Connor hadn't asked because she would've found it difficult to answer him. Not because she didn't know the answer, but because part of the reason for staying was so nonsensical.

How could she explain that she'd stayed because a part of her thought she *deserved* to be punished? After all, she had broken up with Connor because she was worried that he would die someday, and she would be left alone. It sounded so selfish now, but back then, the possibility of her being devastated by his death had been too great a risk for her to take. So basically, she had ended her relationship with Connor because she was a coward.

And how ironic was it that she'd ended up marrying Ashcroft, who had seemed like such a safe, risk-free alternative? Big mistake. Because he hadn't just tried to hurt her. He had tried to *destroy* her, psychologically, bit by bit. There had been moments during her marriage when she didn't know if she would survive another day. After living with that, skydiving and rock climbing didn't look so bad.

"So much for risk aversion," she murmured. From now on, she was going to take the riskiest choice available, every time.

Her cell phone rang and she rushed to grab it, noticed the call number and said, "Grandpa, is everything okay?"

"Just lovely, Maggie. Any day I see sunshine and blue skies is a delightful day. And yourself? How's your day, Maggie, me love?"

Maggie bit back a smile. "Grandpa, did you enjoy a wee dram before you called me?"

"Before I called ye? Ha! Before, during and after's more like it." He laughed so hard he dropped the phone.

"Oh boy," Maggie murmured. It didn't take many wee drams to get Grandpa tanked up and raring to go these days. She was just glad Deidre would be by to make sure he made it to bed and didn't sleep on the couch all night.

The phone was jostled, and then a woman came on the line. "It's Deidre here, Maggie. Angus is doing just fine, not to worry. He's had a wee spot of the angel's tears, but that never hurt a flea."

Maggie chuckled. It sounded as if Deidre might be a bit tipsy, too. They were a pair sometimes. They had probably already changed into their jammies before pouring the first of what sounded like several nightcaps.

"I'm not worried, Deidre," she said. "I know you're taking good care of him."

"Aye, we're coming along just fine." She covered the phone to say something to Grandpa, then came back on the line. "How's my boy treating you?"

"He's a perfect gentleman," Maggie assured her, but her mind instantly raced to a vision of Connor and her, making sweet love last night. She decided she wouldn't be sharing that anecdote with Connor's mother.

Maggie would always be grateful to Deidre for welcoming her back to Point Cairn instead of shutting her out. She had a wonderful open heart and Maggie loved her for it.

"Now you've got the big dance coming up," Deidre continued. "And I know Connor is so looking forward to dancing with you. I hope you two have a beautiful time together."

Maggie frowned. Maybe it was the wee dram speaking, but Deidre sounded almost weepy with happiness. Maggie hated to burst her bubble, but nothing would come of this week with Connor. Other than business, they had no future together. Even though their long talk the night before had answered some questions, Maggie could still catch glimpses of suspicion in Connor's eyes. He'd spent ten long years feeling betrayed and angry with her, so while these past few days together had been lovely, Maggie didn't see how they could possibly erase the painful past.

Maggie heard her grandfather talking in the background, and Deidre said to him, "Well, of course she's going to the dance. Every girl loves to dance."

Grandpa said something and Deidre laughed. "Oh, pish

tosh, Angus. Children can make such a mountain out of a molehill, can't they?"

Angus's laugh was hearty and Deidre joined him. After a few seconds, she must've realized she was still on the phone. "Maggie? Hello? Are you there?"

"Still here," Maggie said.

"All righty, then. Goodbye, dear."

And she disconnected the call, leaving Maggie staring at the phone in befuddlement.

"All righty, then," she muttered, shaking her head as she slipped the phone into her small bag.

The door opened and Connor walked in, then stopped. "Wow. You look…incredible."

She turned and smiled, ridiculously pleased by the compliment. She kept the mood light, twirling around to show off her pretty dress. "So this will do?"

"Absolutely. I'm a lucky man." With a grin, he walked over and kissed her softly on the cheek. "If I were Jonas Wellstone and saw you walk into the room, I would give you anything you wanted."

She gazed up at him solemnly. "And all I would ask for is that he sign over everything to you."

Connor laughed as he helped her with her jacket. "I believe you just might be our secret weapon."

Eight

She hadn't embarrassed herself yet, Maggie thought, smiling inwardly, but the night was still young.

Other than her self-deprecating attitude, everything was lovely tonight. For the private dinner meeting, Mr. Wellstone had chosen a small but beautiful room that had once been an old wine cellar, with arched brick walls and stained glass windows. Candles enhanced the wrought-iron light fixtures, creating a warm, romantic feel, the perfect setting for an intimate dinner for two.

Unfortunately, there were eleven of them at the table and this meal was strictly business.

And the same could be said for her relationship with Connor. It was strictly business, too, in case she'd forgotten. No matter how wonderful their late nights together had been, they shared too much history, too many past mistakes, to risk calling this short time together anything more than business.

To be fair, though, he'd been wonderfully attentive all evening, so she couldn't complain. She just wished things could be different between them somehow. If only she had made some better choices along the way.

But that was ancient history. It was time to stop whining and apologizing about the past. She wanted to enjoy the evening and the rest of the festival. She wanted to savor every minute spent with Connor. And then she would go home and get on with her life.

"How do you like the wine?" Connor whispered next to her.

"It's wonderful," she murmured, reaching for her glass. "Everything is so nice. What do you think? Is it going well?"

Maggie followed his gaze around the table. Other than his brothers and their dates, the rest of the guests were Wellstone family members. Jonas, his son, Paul, and Paul's wife, Dana, and his daughter, Christy, and her husband, Steve. There were several small conversations occurring at once along with plenty of munching and savoring of the delicious stuffed pastry appetizers. Jake and Paul were debating the results of a recent football game.

Connor grinned at Maggie. "I think Jonas looks pretty happy, don't you?"

Maggie glanced over at the man holding court at the head of the table. "He's a kick, isn't he?"

"He's a great guy," he said quietly. "I wasn't sure I would like him because of all these hoops he was making us jump through, but I'm glad we did this tonight. I think everyone's having a good time."

So far, business had only been discussed on a general level. The state of the industry, the latest gossip, who was making waves, who had burned out. There hadn't been a mention of anything specific about the buyout.

Of course, Maggie hadn't expected any real business to be conducted tonight. The purpose of this get-together was to see if everyone got along and to make sure Jonas Wellstone approved of the MacLaren men well enough to sell them his multimillion-dollar brewery business.

The whole scene should've made Maggie unbearably nervous, but it didn't. After spending so many years faking the social niceties with Ashcroft and his snooty high-society crowd, tonight Maggie was dining with real people who laughed and drank wine and enjoyed food and each other's company. It was such a refreshing change. No wonder she felt so happy.

It dawned on her that this was the first time she'd actually been out with a group of people, *any* people, in over three years. She didn't know whether to laugh or cry at that odd little fact.

"Are you okay?" Connor asked. "You looked a little dazed there for a minute."

"I'm perfect," she said, smiling up at him. "I'm happy to be here. Thank you for including me."

"I'm glad you're here with me," he said simply.

As Maggie took another look around the table, Jonas's daughter, Christy, caught her gaze. "I've met a few successful female brewers, Maggie, but it's still pretty rare, isn't it? How did you get started in this business?"

"My mom and dad owned a brewpub for many years in Point Cairn. The same one the MacLarens own now, by the way."

"Hey, we couldn't let it close down," Connor said in defense of his brothers.

"Absolutely not," she said, chuckling. "Anyway, to supplement the brewpub, my father built a home brewery in our barn and I used to follow him around like a puppy, begging to help him. He would give me odd jobs every day, like sorting bottle caps or sweeping the room. At some point, I wound up doing every job there was to do."

"That's the best way to learn," Jonas declared.

"I agree. So a few years ago, I decided to refurbish the brewery equipment in the barn and try my hand at some of my own formulas. And I think I'm starting to make some pretty good beers."

"She's being modest," Jake said, winking at her. "She's been kicking our asses lately at every contest she enters."

Maggie was stunned, no, *flabbergasted* by Jake's compliment. She didn't know if it meant that he'd changed his opinion of her, or if he was just playing nice for Jonas's sake. She decided to take it as a true compliment and bask in the sweetness of the moment.

Under the table, Connor's hand found hers and squeezed gently, sending shivers up her arm and down her back. She glanced up at him and he flashed her a wicked grin.

She wondered if her desire for him was written all over her face. Did she dare to hope he felt the same way about her? Could she risk losing her heart only to find out he wasn't willing to trust her again? She wanted to believe herself ready to take a big risk, but this one might leave her devastated.

Jonas chuckled, interrupting her fantasy. "Competition is good for all of us. I always say a rising tide lifts all boats."

"True enough," Ian said, nodding in agreement.

"What's your father's name, young lady?" Jonas asked.

"His name was Eli Jameson," she said. "He died when I was thirteen."

"Eli?" Jonas's eyes widened. "You're Eli Jameson's little girl?"

Maggie blinked. "Did you know him?"

"Know him?" He chuckled. "Hell, yes. We were great friends back in the day. We first met at a gathering similar to this one, only not nearly as large or as boisterous. Back then, we were a fairly sedate crowd."

"Dad's always talking about the good old days," Christy said, patting her father's arm fondly.

"I loved those days, too," Maggie said. "I always felt so close to my dad when we were working to accomplish something together."

"Your dad and I were competitors," Jonas said, "but it never seemed to matter which one of us won a medal or a ribbon. We hit it off the first time we met and we stayed friends like that until he died."

"That's so nice," Dana murmured.

Jonas grabbed a bread stick and bit off a small chunk. "Your father was a fine man, Maggie. Quite an athlete, too. I went sailing with him a few times, but I couldn't keep up with him. I don't mind saying he scared the hell out of me a few times. I paid him back by dragging him out to the golf course once or twice, but that wasn't his thing. Too slow moving for him. He was what you might call an adventurer. Always looking for the next big challenge. I was sorry to hear about his death."

"Thank you, Jonas," Maggie said, smiling softly at the older man. "Your words brought him back to life for a few minutes."

"It was my pleasure," he said with a firm nod. "They're good memories."

Maggie gazed up at the wrought-iron light fixture and blinked back tears. "You know, I've always thought of my father as a larger-than-life character. But then I would wonder if that was just my own skewed perspective of a little girl in love with her great big father."

"No, he was that kind of man," Jonas assured her. "You should be very proud of him and the legacy he left behind."

"I am," Maggie said. "Thank you so much."

No one spoke for a moment, until Christy patted her father's strong, weathered hand. "That was a very sweet tribute, Dad."

He squeezed her hand but said nothing.

Maggie broke the silence, anxious to move on from the somber topic of her deceased father. "Paul, Connor tells me that you've started growing grapevines and plan to make wine. How is that coming along?"

"Yes, I've turned traitor to my heritage," he said, and his wife and father both laughed. "I'm having a great time with it. It's similar to brewing in that it's a tricky blend of science and art. But the real bonus for me is that picking grapes is so much more fun than picking hops."

"Not quite as many thorns," his wife added.

Everyone at the table chuckled at that.

"Have you bottled anything yet?" Maggie asked.

"We've scheduled our first official bottling next month at the winery. You know, we're just over the hill in Glen Ellen. You should all come join us for the celebration."

She glanced around at Connor and his brothers, who were grinning, no doubt pleased with Paul's offer.

"We'd love to join you," Connor said, speaking for everyone. "Thanks for the invitation."

Paul's wife Dana spoke up. "We've hired a chef for the winery who serves these fabulous little snacks with the tastings. I'm telling you, it's the most fun we've had in years."

"Sounds like you've got quite a setup," Jake said. "I'm looking forward to our visit."

Maggie suddenly wasn't sure if she was included in that group invitation, even though Paul had been responding to her question. It shouldn't matter. She could drive out to their winery any time she wanted to, but it would be so much nicer to go with this group of people she was starting to consider friends.

"Wineries." Jonas sighed. "Another reason why I'm selling the brewery, boys. My own son is deserting the company."

"Aw, come on Dad," Paul said guiltily.

He grinned. "I'm just teasing you, boy. I'm glad you've found something you enjoy as much as I love my brewing." His gaze slid from Jake to Ian to Connor. "Gentlemen, that's why I insist that whoever buys my company should love this business as much as I do. I don't want some buttoned-down pencil pusher running my plant and pissing off the loyal employees who've worked there all these years. I want someone who walks in every morning and takes a deep breath of that hoppy smell and actually gets excited at the possibilities."

Maggie smiled, knowing exactly what the old man meant.

"Who knows what can happen when you blend all those bitter herbs and malts together?" Jonas's eyes sparkled as he spoke. "Why, throw in a slice of lemon peel or some odd bit of vegetation and you could come up with something completely new that might dominate the industry for the next five years. I'm telling you, if you can't appreciate the scent, the shades, the taste, the…" He paused, then chuckled. "Hell, I sound like I'm talking about a woman."

Everybody laughed, but Jonas laughed the hardest. "I'm talking about beer, gentlemen. And ladies, of course. I love this damn business."

"Right there with you, Jonas," Connor said, raising his glass in a sentimental toast.

"It really is the best thing in the world, isn't it?" Maggie said dreamily. "At the end of the day, when you've hosed down the brewing station and steam-cleaned the pipes and you've tapped off your latest keg and you're hot and sweaty and you can finally sit down on the porch and taste the day's batch while you relax and watch the sun go down? I don't think there's a better moment that captures the essence of beer making than that one."

"Dang, Maggie May." Jonas grinned and she could see a sparkle in his eyes. He held up his half-empty wineglass for another toast. "That's pure poetry."

She laughed at her new nickname and held up her glass to meet his. "Here's to special moments."

"I'll drink to that," he said jovially, and chugged down what was left of his wine.

"I was right," Connor said later that night after they'd made love.

"About what?"

"You turned out to be our secret weapon," he said, reminding her of his comment earlier that night.

She gave him a puzzled look. She was stretched out on her back, her head propped on a pillow. He lay on his side, facing her, his hand resting on her smooth stomach.

"I don't know about that," she said as she absently ran her fingers along his shoulder and down his arm. "But it was fun to hear Jonas talk about my dad."

"Everyone enjoyed hearing about him," he said, earning a smile from her. "It was a good evening."

"Did you get an inkling of Jonas's decision yet?"

"Jake talked to Paul briefly while we were walking back to the hotel. "He thinks we've got a lock on the deal."

"That's wonderful."

"Yeah. I won't count any chickens yet, but I think there's a strong possibility that he'll sell to us. There's plenty of work to do in the meantime, but it would be a real coup to take over Wellstone."

"I'll say."

It struck Connor that this was an odd sort of "pillow talk" conversation to be having with a woman, but it was one more indication of how comfortable he was around Maggie.

And that wasn't necessarily a good thing, he thought suddenly, unable to keep his old suspicions from cropping back up. Yes, Maggie had given him a simple explanation for why she'd left him all those years ago. Connor completely believed that she had feared for his safety back then.

But had she truly explained the fact that, before he could even grasp that she was truly gone, he'd received the news that she had married another man? Okay, maybe she was telling the truth when she said she'd been awash in grief and made a really bad decision. But he had to wonder how "in love" with Connor she'd really been to turn around and do something like that.

It didn't matter. What was he doing, thinking about this stuff when he had a warm, beautiful woman in his bed? He should be celebrating the fact that his plan to get her into bed had succeeded. Now he could relax and enjoy the moment.

It wasn't as if they had mentioned anything about getting back together. This was a one-time deal. When the week was over, he would hand her a check and go back to his life.

He ignored the wave of melancholy that that thought brought on.

Hell, there was a simple explanation for all this angst he was feeling. He hadn't been with another woman in…gads, had it been six months? No wonder he was reeling from all these unwanted emotions. But it was about time to snap out of it, he thought. A beautiful woman was pressing her lush body against him and he had the unrelenting urge to bury himself inside her. Again. And again.

And why not? Shouldn't he be making up for lost time? And while he was on the subject, why shouldn't he and Maggie keep on doing it, as long as the sex was good? And it was definitely good. Hell, it was world class. So why should they go their separate ways once the festival ended? Connor wondered. They lived in the same town, so why not continue to enjoy each other's company? It didn't have to be a big deal. Nothing special or permanent. Or complicated. Why couldn't it just be for fun? They could be friends with benefits. Nothing wrong with that.

For now, he tugged her onto her side facing him, then rolled back until she was on top of him, straddling his solid length.

"Oh, how did I get here?" she said, teasing him.

"Magic," he whispered, and lifted her up until he could slide into her.

She sank onto him, moaning in pleasure. And there was no more pillow talk for the rest of the night.

* * *

At breakfast Friday morning, Maggie watched Connor scan his email as he finished his coffee. He was dressed more formally than usual in a black suit, white shirt and rich burgundy power tie. He looked so good Maggie wanted to rip off his clothes and have her way with him.

He set his empty coffee cup on the dining table and stood. "I've got two meetings back to back this afternoon and the second one will probably run late, so I'll meet you at the gala by eight o'clock."

Maggie stood, too, and adjusted his tie. "Connor, I already told you I'm not going to the gala."

"Let's not go through this again, Maggie," he said. "You'll be there. It's required."

She made a face. "No, it's not. I told you I didn't want to go. The truth is, I don't like these sorts of events. I didn't even bring the right kind of dress to wear."

"So what?" he said, snapping his phone into its case and shoving it into his suit pocket. "You can wear any one of the dresses you've already worn this week."

"No, I can't. The gala is formal. Nothing I have is suitable."

"I'm not dressing formally," he said, glancing down at his suit.

"Oh, please." Maggie's laugh sounded slightly desperate. "That suit's got to be worth five thousand dollars. I think you can get away with wearing it. But I'll be expected to wear a gown and I don't have one."

"You should've thought of that before now," he said as he walked to the door. "I don't care what you wear, but I expect to see you there."

"But—" She ran after him to the door. "Connor, please. I can't—"

He grabbed the doorknob, then stopped and turned.

"This was always part of our deal. It's not optional. It's business."

"But I don't dance."

"I don't care," he said heatedly.

"Why are you making such a big deal about it?"

"Because I can." He yanked her close and crushed her lips with his. She moaned and he softened the kiss, sweeping his tongue over hers. When he finally let her go, her knees wobbled from the pleasure of his kiss. "Please, Maggie," he said, touching his forehead to hers. "Please, I want you there with me."

"Big bully," she muttered, and touched her fingers to her lips to make sure that kiss hadn't been a dream.

"Coward," he whispered, then kissed her again, briefly and softly this time, and walked out, letting the door close behind him.

She absorbed the silence for a moment, then flopped onto the couch. "Now what?"

She wandered the convention floor all morning, listening to other speakers and catching up with some of the new acquaintances she'd made this week. She had lunch alone overlooking the marina, but instead of enjoying the view, she agonized over the gala. Connor simply didn't understand. Why would he? It was no big deal. Except it was, to Maggie.

Staring out at the sparkling blue water, she sighed. The thought of attending the gala should've filled her with excitement, but Maggie was filled with dread instead. It sounded ridiculously melodramatic to say she might not survive the evening, but that was exactly what she was afraid of.

The last gala event she had attended was the Hospital Society's Black & White Ball, back in Boston. Her ex-husband had been the chairman of the event and it was a huge success. He should have been flushed with happiness, but that was so *not* Alan. Maggie still wasn't exactly sure what she had done to set him off. Had she been too effusive in congratulating him? Had she danced too close to one of his lackeys? Had she spilled something on her ball gown?

Whatever small offense she'd shown, Alan was apparently intent on making sure it didn't go unnoticed, even if it meant exposing their unhappy relationship to the world.

Leaving her in the middle of the dance floor, Alan had approached the bandleader and ordered him to stop the music. He had an important announcement to make.

"My wife is a whore," he had announced to the crème de la crème of Boston society. He didn't stop there, but Maggie refused to play back the entire tawdry speech in her mind. And later that night in the foyer of their home, he struck her physically for the first time, smacking her face so hard that she fell and hit her head against the hard surface of a marble statue, and passed out.

Two days later, after her headache had subsided and she'd regained some strength, Maggie snuck out to a pay phone and called a lawyer to begin divorce proceedings. She knew it would be a vicious battle and she prayed she would survive it. Her prayers were answered when her surly mother-in-law died a few days later and Alan divorced her instead.

Maggie had never told another soul about Alan's physical attack. How could she, when she could touch her cheek and still feel the physical blow he'd delivered? And if she closed her eyes, she could still experience the rush of utter mortification she'd felt on that dance floor as her husband destroyed her in front of everyone she knew.

She would never allow herself to be so humiliated again. Even if it meant she would never stand on another dance floor again.

"Would you like anything else?" the waiter asked.

Maggie flinched. She'd been so buried in the past she'd forgotten where she was. She quickly recovered and smiled. "No, just the check, thank you."

She returned to the convention floor, but after stirring up all those unhappy memories, she was unable to enjoy herself. She went back up to the suite to take a nap, but she couldn't sleep. She was awash in misery and clueless as to why she couldn't just flick away the past, shape up, straighten her shoulders and power through this dilemma.

After fixing herself a cup of tea, she sat by the window and stared out at the calming view of ocean water and windswept sky.

The fact was, she wanted to be with Connor, even though she dreaded attending the gala. So brushing aside the dread, she focused on her present predicament. She didn't have a dress!

She mentally sifted through the practical issues before her, as if they were written on a list she could check off. First, she didn't have a proper gown or even an ultrafancy cocktail dress to wear because she'd given away all of her dress-up clothes when she left Ashcroft. For good reason. They all reminded her of horrible, embarrassing times spent with her ex-husband.

Second, now that she'd given everything away, she couldn't afford to run out and buy something new, especially something so fancy. Not to mention the shoes and jewelry to wear with it.

Third, when she first made the deal with Connor, she honestly hadn't thought it would matter whether she showed up for the gala or not. But they had grown so close during the past week, she didn't want to disappoint him.

But that brought her to issue number four. The real problem. She hated going to formal events. Hated dancing. Feared what would happen if she did the wrong thing. Over time, the fear and hate had grown into a phobia. She'd spent way too many years attending monthly charity balls and society dances with Ashcroft, trying to impress his mother and all their rich, snooty friends, knowing that no matter what she did, it was always going to be the wrong thing.

Besides the big ugly result of the final event with Ashcroft, there had been plenty of other nasty repercussions that had occurred after she'd made some miniscule faux pas at a society dance. Maggie cringed and rubbed her arms to calm the shivers she felt. She refused to dwell on the various creative, nonphysical ways her ex-husband had made her pay for her innocent social foibles.

"This is ridiculous," she whispered. She was obviously still suffering from Post-Ashcroft Distress Syndrome, which probably wasn't a real disease, but it should've been.

She really needed to snap out of it.

But she couldn't. Because of issue number five. This gala tonight was actually important to her career. There would be people at tonight's event who were vital industry contacts, business professionals, the very people she wanted to impress so badly. But how could she? She had nothing to wear. Which brought her right back to issue number one.

It was a vicious circle and Maggie's head was spinning out of control.

She yawned, exhausted from worrying so much. Sitting down on the couch, she leaned back against one of the soft pillows and tried again to close her eyes for a few minutes.

The doorbell rang, waking her up. Disoriented, she had to stare at the clock for ten seconds before it registered that she'd slept for almost two hours. So much for worrying that she wouldn't be able to fall asleep.

She ran to the door and pulled it open.

"Delivery for Ms. Jameson," the bellman said, and handed her a large white box.

What was this? She was almost afraid to take it from him, but she did.

"Thank you," she murmured, and quickly searched for a few dollars to give as a tip. Then she closed the door and set the box on the coffee table. It carried the logo of a well-known, expensive women's store. She stared at it for several minutes, unsure what to do. Was it really for her? Maybe it was something Connor had ordered for one of his judging seminars.

"You're being silly." She double-checked the box and saw her name on a label on the side, just as the bellman had said.

Finally she settled down on the couch and slowly pulled off the top and saw…a blanket of tissue covering the contents. Okay, that wasn't too intimidating. She waded through the paper and finally found the real contents of the box.

"Oh my." It was pink. That was the first surprise. It was also soft. And beautiful. She lifted the dress out of the box and held it up to her, then ran over and stared at herself in the mirror. It was strapless, with beading all over the bodice, to the waist. From there, layers of soft pink chiffon flowed in a soft column to the floor. It was formal, but sexy. And sweet. And perfect. She'd never seen a more beautiful dress.

It complemented her skin tone and her hair. It was simply ideal. Almost as if it had been made for her.

There were shoes in the box, as well. She slipped her foot into one of them and was amazed that it fit her. At the bottom of the box, she found a small pouch that held diamond earrings and a necklace.

She didn't have to guess where all of this had come from.

"Connor," she whispered, and felt a spurt of happiness that he would do something so thoughtful.

"Wait a minute," she said, as reality sank in. Why would

he ever dare to buy her a dress after she'd spent most of their dinner the other night complaining about Ashcroft doing the same thing?

So who could've bought her this beautiful dress? Connor was the only person who knew that she—

Her cell phone rang and she ran to answer it.

"Maggie love."

"Grandpa. Is everything all right?"

"Fine and dandy," he said. "And are you having a good time?"

"I am, Grandpa. Are you feeling well today?"

"Fit as a fiddle," he said, and she could hear him patting his belly.

It was an old joke. He was tall and thin and barely had a belly to pat.

Someone giggled in the background.

"Grandpa, who's there with you?"

"It's our Deidre, making dinner."

"That's nice. And how are the goats?"

"They're a delight as always," he said "But how are you, Maggie love? We wanted to call and check. Is everything hunky-dory?"

"Everything's fine," Maggie said, touched that he was so concerned. It was unusual for her grandfather to use the telephone unless he was forced to, so maybe this was Deidre's influence.

"And how will you spend your evening, lass?" he asked. "Any special plans?"

"Grandpa, don't you remember I told you…" She paused. Something was wrong. Every time she'd talked to her grandfather during the past week, he had asked her about the dance. So why was he…? Her eyes narrowed in on the pink dress. "Grandpa, did you send me something today?"

"Och, aye, lass!" he shouted excitedly. "So it arrived?"

"She got it, then?" Deidre said, clear enough for Maggie to hear. "And does it fit?"

Maggie plopped down on the couch, speechless.

"Are you there, lass?"

"Did she hang up?"

"I'm here," she whispered. "Grandpa, why? You know I don't dance anymore."

"That's just something you tell yourself, lass," he said softly. "For protection."

She blinked at his words, but before she could respond, Deidre grabbed the phone. "Now, don't blame your grandpa for speaking out of school, but I've heard a thing or two about a thing or two."

Maggie smiled indulgently as Deidre made her point. "I'll tell you a secret, Maggie. I still have the picture of you and Connor at your high school prom. Such a pretty pair, you were. You danced all night and I know you loved it. You love to dance, Maggie. I don't know why or how you decided to stop loving it, but maybe you should decide to start again."

"Is it that simple?" Maggie wondered aloud.

"Most things are," Deidre said philosophically. "And as long as I'm giving out free advice, I think it's high time you closed the door on the past and started living in the *now*. Live for yourself. Choose for yourself, Maggie. Now here's your grandpa."

Choose for herself? Maggie stared at the telephone and began to pace back and forth across the room. Choose for herself? But every time she'd made choices, she'd made mistakes.

But so what? she argued. Was she never supposed to do anything fun or risky, ever again? She might as well live in a glass bubble!

But making choices was the same as taking risks, and taking risks meant that she might get hurt. Or worse.

But if she didn't take the risk, if she didn't go to the dance, she knew she would hurt much worse. And Connor would be hurt, as well.

So it seemed she had no choice.

Oh, good grief! Of course she had a choice. She could choose to go to the dance and have fun with Connor.

Exhausted from arguing with herself, Maggie slid down onto the couch.

Angus came back on the line. "No more guff now, lass. Tell me, do you like the dress?"

"It's beautiful, Grandpa, but you can't afford to—"

"Och, there'll be none o' that," he argued. "I've a little something tucked away for a rainy day, and Deidre chipped in a bit."

"I'll pay you both back."

"You'll not pay us back," Grandpa grumbled.

Deidre grabbed the phone. "You'll pay us back by dancing your little toes off with my son. Now, you have a fancy dance to prepare for. Go. Get off the phone and go."

"Yes, ma'am," Maggie said, and laughed as she disconnected the call.

The elevator moved slowly on the trip down to the lobby, giving Maggie more time to worry about every little thing that could go wrong. She caught a glimpse of her reflection in the elevator's mirrored wall, and it helped remind herself that there were plenty of things that were going to go just right.

She had made a pact with herself that from now on, the past would stay in the past. It was time to forgive herself for the mistakes she'd made back then. She was ready to move forward, not backward.

And tonight she was going to dance. With Connor, of course, and with anyone else who asked. Deidre was right. Maggie refused to sit in a corner anymore, worrying whether she might make a mistake or do the wrong thing. It was a risk, but she was ready to take it.

Two hours ago, she had refused to even try on the pink dress because the very thought of walking into the dance tonight made her queasy. Would she have flashbacks? Would someone criticize her for laughing too much? Would people sneer at the way she danced? Would they think her dress was too sexy? Too sparkly? Too pink?

There would be hors d'oeuvres and desserts served at the dance, too. What if she spilled something? What if she used the wrong fork? Because Ashcroft had once punished her for using the wrong fork.

"Good grief," she muttered. The wrong fork? Seriously? Who the hell cared?

She began to laugh at herself, so hard that tears came to her eyes. Then she tried to picture Connor sniveling about the wrong fork, and she laughed even harder.

It was ludicrous. And worse, it was tearing her apart inside and destroying her hard-won self-confidence. So really, wasn't it about time she drop-kicked her asinine ex-husband and his bony old mother out of her memory banks? Yes!

"And take your wrong fork with you!" she said in a loud voice, shaking her fist in the air.

Recalling her minitirade, Maggie giggled again. It was a good thing she was alone in the elevator. Otherwise, she might've received more than a few strange looks from her fellow passengers.

Nine

"Where's your date?"

Connor glanced at his brother while he casually sipped a beer, refusing to reveal how concerned he was over the subject of Jake's question. "She'll be here."

"You sure?"

"Yes," he said with a nonchalance he didn't feel.

"Good," Jake said, and grinned. "Think she'll dance with me?"

He scowled at his brother. "No."

Jake looked affronted. "Why the hell not?"

"Because you were a jerk to her."

"That's ancient history," he said, brushing away Connor's comment. "I thought we got along really swell at dinner the other night."

"Swell, huh?" Connor looked at him sideways. "That's because I warned you to be nice to her."

"That's not why," Jake insisted. "She was great. Talkative, interesting, fun. She loves the business, so she's got some smarts. Besides, if you can forgive her, who am I to judge? And Jonas loved her, so that counts for something."

"Yeah, it does." Connor refused to mention the twinge of affection he felt at hearing his brother's kind words. Instead he kept scanning the room for the exasperating woman he wanted to have standing by his side at that moment.

The place was filled with old friends and business acquaintances, wealthy competitors and a few enemies, all decked out in their fanciest attire. The men were in tuxedos or black suits and most of the women wore gowns. And they were all working the crowd. This was business, after all.

There were occasional flashes of light as the local paparazzi caught people on camera out in the wide-open foyer. The photos would eventually appear in the various industry magazines and websites, so everyone took it in good-natured fun.

But still there was no Maggie. Damn it, was she seriously planning to stand him up? But wait, could he blame her? She honestly didn't want to come tonight and he had done everything to bully her into it. And that was after she'd been so honest with him, telling him about her vicious ex-husband's behavior.

"You're a moron," he muttered miserably.

"Just so you know," Jake continued blithely, "I'm okay with you and her getting together."

Connor's eyebrow quirked. "And what's that supposed to mean?"

"It means, you know, if you wanted to actually date her, I'd be okay with it."

Connor placed his hand over his heart. "That means everything to me."

Jake laughed out loud. "Yeah, right. I know it matters, so I'm just saying, Maggie's A-okay in my book."

"You're wrong," Connor said, grinning. "It doesn't matter to me."

"Of course it matters," Jake persisted, only half kidding. "I'm the head of the family, so it's a very special occasion when I bestow my blessing upon you."

Ian overheard him as he walked up to join them. "Head *jackass* of the family, maybe."

Connor chuckled. "Good one."

"So, what were you two blathering about?" Ian asked as he sipped from a glass of red wine.

Jake pointed to Connor. "I was just telling him I'm okay with him and Maggie hooking up."

Ian smirked at Connor. "I'm sure you appreciated those heartfelt words."

"Oh, you bet," Connor said. "You know how much I look up to Jake and hang on his every word."

"Go ahead and give me grief," Jake said loftily. "But I'm not too big a person to admit when I'm wrong. I take back what I said about Maggie. She's a lovely woman and she's obviously still in love with you, so I wish you two many years of happiness together."

"Whoa," Connor said, carefully swallowing the gulp of beer he'd almost choked on. "Slow down, dude. Who said anything about, you know, whatever the hell you're talking about?"

Ian ignored Connor's protest. "As much as I hate to utter the words, I have to agree with Jake. You and Maggie have a really nice vibe together. So don't screw it up."

"Yeah," Jake chimed in. "Just make sure she sticks around this time."

"It wasn't my fault she left," he groused under his breath. But it was a halfhearted protest. He was no longer opposed to the idea of being with Maggie, even as he pretended to be so in front of his brothers. He'd been doing a lot of thinking over the past few days and he'd come to the realization that maybe he did have some culpability, after all. It was hard to admit it because he'd spent so many years blaming things all on Maggie. But after the other night when they'd talked it out, he could see that he'd done plenty to drive her crazy back then.

With the arrogance of youth, he'd carelessly ignored the warning signs she'd been giving him all along. Now he could kick himself for not paying closer attention. And while he was kicking himself, he would gladly give himself the boot for not going after her in the first place. But his pride had gotten in the way and he'd ended up wasting all those years without her.

So now that he couldn't wait to see her, where the hell was she? Not only did he miss her, but he also had some important news to give her. He wasn't sure she would appreciate him sticking his nose into her business, but that was too damn bad. She would want to hear this.

Earlier that day, Connor and his brothers had spent an hour with their longtime local banker, Dave, to discuss some hometown investments. After the meeting had wrapped up, Connor had pulled Dave aside to ask if he knew the reason why his bank had turned down Maggie's loan application.

At first Dave had been reluctant to say anything. There were privacy issues involved, naturally.

"Come on, Dave," Connor had cajoled. "We've known each other since grammar school. You can be sure that anything you tell me won't leave this room."

"Hell, Connor." He scraped his fingers across his thinning scalp.

"Look," Connor said, trying another tack, "the truth is, I'm floating her a loan, so I'd like to know if she's good for paying it back."

"Of course she is," Dave insisted. "But you know how things are these days. Her credit report came back with one black mark on it and with all our red tape, the loan wasn't allowed to go through."

"A black mark? From where?"

"Some company back East."

"Remember the name?" Connor knew that their local bank was small enough that even as executive vice president, Dave would still go over each of the loans himself.

Dave thought for a moment. "Cargrove? Casgrow?"

"Cosgrove?" Connor said.

"That's it," Dave exclaimed. "Apparently she ran up

quite a debt with them, although I've got to admit I've never even heard of them. Must be some regional store or something."

"Or something," Connor muttered.

"I felt really bad, turning her down," Dave continued. "And Maggie was devastated. She walked out of my office without even asking for her credit information."

Connor wasn't surprised, but it broke his heart to hear it. Maggie's self-esteem had taken such a beating, it figured she would simply blame herself for her inability to get a bank loan, not even suspecting that her lousy ex-husband, Alan Cosgrove, had gone and screwed up her credit rating, just to twist the knife in one more time for good measure.

Connor really wanted to meet this psychopathic dirtbag and smash his face in. He had every intention of doing it, but that happy moment would have to wait.

The Big Band orchestra had been playing softly for the past half hour as people streamed into the ballroom, but now the conductor tapped his baton and the music burst into high gear. Couples began to fill the dance floor. The lines at all four bars were growing and the crowd in front of the appetizers and dessert tables were now three deep.

So where the hell was Maggie?

"I'll be back," Connor told his brothers, but he hadn't taken ten steps before he ran into Lucinda.

"Hi, Connor," she said breathlessly, taking hold of his arm. "Don't you look dashing tonight. Oh, but you're not leaving, are you?"

"Hey, Lucinda. I've gotta run out for a minute, but I'll be back."

"Oh, good." She smiled shyly. "I expect to dance with you at least once tonight."

"Sure thing," he said in a rush, then stopped abruptly. "Sorry. Don't know where my manners went. You look really nice, too, Lucinda."

"Thank you, Connor," she said, beaming at him. "That's sweet of you."

"I'll be back."

"Okay," she said, but he was already halfway across the room.

But before he could escape, he was flagged down by Bob Milburn, the mayor of Point Cairn, who wanted to discuss the amount the MacLarens planned to contribute to the annual Christmas parade and party the town held every year. Connor had to endure five long minutes of mindless chatter before Jake and Ian finally rescued him.

"Sorry to interrupt you two, Ian said briskly. "But we need to pull Connor away to discuss some family business."

"Sure thing," Bob said amiably. "See you boys around."

As soon as the mayor was out of hearing range, Connor let out the breath he'd been holding. "Damn, I thought he would never stop talking."

"We saw you floundering," Ian said.

Jake grinned. "You looked pretty desperate."

"I was." He glanced around the room again, then checked his wristwatch. "Listen, I've really got to go find Maggie."

Jake grabbed Connor's arm to keep him from dashing off. "That won't be necessary."

"Whoa," Ian whispered.

"Guess you were right, bro," Jake murmured. "She did show up."

Connor turned and spotted Maggie standing on the threshold of the farthest doorway from where they stood.

"Wow," Jake said reverently.

"About time she showed up," Connor muttered, then couldn't say another word, just continued to stare as she walked into the room. She was a vision in pale pink, so sexy and gorgeous he wasn't sure if she was real or just a hallucination of his addled mind.

Her strapless gown clung to her stunning breasts in

a gravity-defying miracle of sparkling pink and crystal beads. At her waist, the beads disappeared and the dress flowed in a wispy column to the floor. Her gorgeous hair was held up by some pins with a few tendrils allowed to hang loose and curl around her shoulders

She looked like a sexy angel, and never more beautiful than at this moment. And that was saying a lot, Connor thought, because she always looked beautiful to him.

Connor continued to watch her as he sauntered across the ballroom to meet her. As he got closer, his insides constricted at the memory of her moaning in pleasure as he filled her completely last night. His jaw tightened as he tried to estimate exactly how long he would have to endure this party before he could take her back to their bed, where he would soon have her naked and whimpering with need.

"Glad you could make it," he said when he finally reached her.

"I'm sorry I'm late," she said, tiptoeing up to kiss his cheek. "Forgive me?"

The orchestra began to play a jazz standard, and without another word, Connor took her hand and led her out to the dance floor, where he pulled her into his arms and began to sway to the music. When Maggie rested her head on his shoulder, he was certain that nothing had ever felt more right.

After a full minute, he leaned his head back and gazed down at her. "It was worth the wait, Maggie."

An hour later, Connor felt trapped by his own success. Maggie hadn't stopped dancing, not once. It seemed that every man Connor had introduced her to during the week now wanted to dance with her. First it was Jonas, then his son, Paul, then big Johnny from the judges' room. Hell, even Pete from Stink Bug Brewery had claimed a dance.

Connor had danced, as well, with Lucinda and Paul

Wellstone's wife, Dana, and two women he barely knew who were friends of Jake's.

He was so ready to blow this party off, grab Maggie and go back upstairs. But it was not to be. No, instead he got caught up in some off-the-wall conversation with Jonas about fruit-flavored ales. The old man was waxing on about boysenberries and ten minutes had passed before Connor noticed that Maggie was standing on the sidelines talking to someone. He couldn't see the man's face, so he shifted his stance until he could get a look at the guy. And he didn't like what he saw.

"Damn it," he muttered. "What's that about?" Maggie was talking to Ted Blake. It couldn't be a good thing.

"Something's wrong," Jonas declared. "You suddenly look like you just ate a bad-tasting bug."

"I'm sorry, Jonas," he said, "but I think I'd better go rescue Maggie."

Jonas's eyes scanned the room and then narrowed in on Maggie and Ted. He nodded slowly. "Good idea, son. That boy's nothing but trouble."

Connor's stomach tightened all over again as he watched her laughing and joking with the guy who had tried to destroy MacLaren. When Ted leaned in and whispered something in her ear, Connor's vision blurred in anger.

He thought he'd warned her about Ted Blake after he saw her talking to him the other day on the convention floor. But now he realized that he'd simply glossed over it at the time. And after that one time, he hadn't seen the guy all week. It was another reason why he'd had such a good time at the festival this week. No Ted Blake to deal with.

"Maggie."

She whirled around. "Oh, Connor, there you are. You've probably met Ted before, but we were just—"

"Yeah, we've met," Connor said curtly, and grabbed her hand. "Come on, babe, time to go."

"But…okay. Nice to see you again, Ted."

"Sure thing, Maggie," Ted drawled. "Maybe we'll talk again when you're not in such a hurry."

"Don't count on it," Connor muttered as he pulled Maggie closer and walked faster.

"Connor, please, can we walk a little slower? My feet are starting to whimper from all the dancing."

"Sorry, baby," he said, slowing down. "I just wanted to get you away from him. The faster the better."

"But why?" She glanced over her shoulder to get a last look at Ted. "He seems like a nice enough guy. A little bit quirky, but—"

"He's the furthest thing from a nice guy you'll meet here." Frowning, he added, "I can't tell you who to talk to or who to do business with, Maggie. But I would highly recommend that you stay as far away from Ted Blake as possible."

She studied his face for a moment, then nodded. "All right. I've never seen you react so negatively to anyone before."

"He tried to ruin us when we were first starting out," Connor said flatly. "Lucky for us, his reputation preceded him and a few of the people he talked to in his crusade to smear us didn't believe him. But a few of them did, and we had some shaky moments there."

"What a rat!" Maggie said, and suddenly wondered if Ted had known she was attending the festival with Connor when he first approached her. Did he think he could damage her business, as well? She remembered some of the odd questions he'd asked her that first time they met. Her shoulders slumped. "You'd think I'd recognize the species after living with one for so many years."

"The thing about rats is, they're really good at pretending they're something other than a rat."

"Too true," she murmured, shaking her head in dismay.

He pulled her closer, wrapping his arm around her as they walked. "Don't worry about it. There's a lot more to the story of Ted, but I'll save it for another time. Not tonight."

"Okay." She paused, then added, "But I feel like such a fool for buying in to his act. I thought he was sort of an odd bird, but he seemed harmless enough. Is there any chance he might've changed over the years?"

"No," he said flatly. "He's always been a lying snake, and the fact that he struck up a conversation with you is a sure sign that he hasn't changed one bit. He knows you're here with me. That's the only reason why he approached you in the first place."

"And here I thought it was my sparkling wit that attracted him to me."

Connor stopped and stared at her. Then he rubbed his hand across his jawline. "Hell, Maggie. I'm sorry. I didn't mean it the way it came out. Any man in that room tonight would be damn lucky to breathe the same air as you."

"I was just teasing you." She beamed a smile at him and wound her arm through his. "Let's forget about Ted. I just want to go upstairs with you."

"Sounds good to me."

"Mm, and I can't wait to take off my shoes."

"This might help," Connor said, and swept her up in his arms.

"I could really get used to this," she murmured, wrapping her arms securely around his neck.

So could I, Connor thought, but didn't say the words aloud as he carried her snugly in his arms across the lobby to the elevators.

It was crazy, Maggie thought as they lay in bed together. They'd spent almost every night of the past week making love with each other, but still she wanted more. Would this need she felt for him ever diminish?

They'd raced from the elevator to the hotel suite, and after tearing off their clothes, they'd fallen into bed and immediately devoured each other.

Now, just as she was slipping into sleep, Connor reached for her again. And she couldn't resist him.

She stirred and saw him, saw the sweet desire reflected in his eyes and knew he could see it in hers, as well. Knew he wanted the same thing in that moment that she did. It awakened her, filling her with so much love she could barely wait to hold him inside her again.

Purely and simply, she had fallen irrevocably in love with him and there was no escaping the truth. Maybe she'd known all along that this was where she would end up from the first moment she walked into his office and saw him sitting at his desk.

She'd first gone to see him thinking she would be unfazed by his charm. She had known she was taking a risk but was certain she'd gotten over him years ago. But clearly, she was wrong. The passion was still there, as real and palpable as it ever had been, even after ten long years.

She adored Connor's hands, loved the way he touched her, the way he stroked her everywhere, the way he continuously awakened her body to such pleasure and desire. And she prayed he would never stop.

He slid lower to taste her and with the first sensation of his mouth on her, she gasped and arched into him. Then her mind emptied of all thought and she could only feel and enjoy. His fingers and lips brought her to the brink of ecstasy, only to reel her back and start all over again. When he swept in with his tongue and flicked at her very core, she shuddered as a sudden climax erupted, threatening to engulf her in a pool of need and yearning.

"Again," he murmured, his voice edgy with hunger.

"But...I don't...I can't..."

His gaze locked on hers and she shivered with need. "For me, Maggie."

"Yes," she whispered.

"I want to watch you," he said in a raw, throaty whisper. "I want to feel you tremble in my arms. I want to see your eyes turn dark with pleasure." And he moved his fingers in a staccato rhythm that drove her straight to the edge of rapture and then beyond as she shattered in his hands.

Seconds—or was it minutes—later, he eased her onto her stomach and covered her with his muscled body. His flesh pressed against hers as he kissed her shoulder. And in a heartbeat, she was enflamed with need. She wanted him, wanted everything he had to give her, almost as if she hadn't just fallen apart in his arms minutes earlier.

He trailed kisses along her spine, stroked her as he lowered himself down to plant kisses on her behind, then continued down her thighs, licking and nibbling and exploring every inch of skin until she was breathless again.

"Please, Connor." She wanted to see him, watch him, kiss him. She started to roll over, but he stroked her back, silently urging her to stay this way awhile longer. He kissed her again at the base of her neck and began the tender onslaught all over again.

Maggie sighed, then moaned as his fingers moved to stroke her more intimately again. Then he suddenly shifted, lifted her pelvis and shifted her hips to allow him entrance. When he thrust himself into her, she gasped for air. He was hard and solid as he delved deeper, filling her completely until she was sure he had touched her soul.

She met his urgent movements with her own, could hear him gasping for breath, could feel his heated body scorching her skin, and hoped this feeling would never go away, prayed that this moment would never end.

Suddenly he stopped and she almost collapsed, but he

held her steady. He pulled himself away from her and she almost cried until he gently rolled her over onto her back.

"I have to look at you," he said, simply, and instantly thrust himself inside her. She gasped, and then immediately felt complete again with him sheathed within her.

He moved faster now, plunging deeper, thrusting harder, taking her along on a frantic ride to an inexorable climax that had her screaming his name within mere seconds.

Connor tightened his hold on her, driving into her. She could feel the immense coil of tension rise within him and stretch to the breaking point. Only then did he shout out her name and follow her into blissful oblivion.

Ten

Connor woke up the next morning with a beautiful warm woman snuggled beside him. His first impulse was to wake her up slowly, kiss by kiss, touch by touch, until she welcomed him gladly into her heated core once again.

Despite his rampant erection, he couldn't do it. She looked so peaceful Connor didn't have the heart to wake her. And he figured, from now on, they had all the time in the world to spend pleasuring each other.

For now, he climbed out of bed, careful not to disturb her, and prepared for the day. The awards ceremony would be early this evening and he still had some final round judging to finish before noon.

He was reading the sports section and drinking his second cup of coffee from room service when he received a text from Jake. Emergency. Meet us in judges room immediately. Come alone.

Maggie awoke slowly, happy but exhausted from their lovemaking the night before. She glanced across the bed and found it empty, so Connor was already up and out of bed. She must have overslept, she thought, stretching languidly. Every muscle in her body was groaning, but it was so worth it. No pain, no gain, right? She chuckled lazily and glanced at the clock.

"Oh dear." She really had overslept. She didn't hear Connor in the bathroom, so she walked out into the living room to check whether he was still eating breakfast. The suite was deserted, so she knew he must have left for the festival floor.

It took her a few seconds to remember what day this was. Saturday. The day of the final judging. Tonight was the awards ceremony. She needed to kick herself into gear.

Today would also be the busiest day of the festival with members of the general public coming in droves. She would need extra energy to fight the crowds, but all that was left of Connor's breakfast was a piece of leftover toast and one last cup of coffee. She grabbed them both, then raced to shower and dry her hair. She decided to dress a little more casually in capris, a short linen jacket and a pair of colorful sneakers.

Still hungry, she stopped at the coffee kiosk in the lobby and bought herself a quick breakfast burrito and a latte.

Then she went directly down to the judges' room to find Connor. She knew she wouldn't be allowed inside during the final judging round, but she just hoped she could see his face.

The doors to the hall were closed and the outer foyer was deserted. Maggie glanced around, looking for Johnny, but he was nowhere to be found, either.

She finished her latte and tossed the cup in a trash can, then decided to make a run to the ladies' room while she had a few minutes.

She slipped into one of the stalls, hung her tote bag on the hook and had to smile. She'd been in here before, the other day when she'd been too afraid to confront Sarah. She had dashed to the safety of the bathroom stall like a helpless ninny, but never again, she vowed. She was fed up with being afraid. She would never hide from confrontation again.

Before she could exit the stall, the outer bathroom door opened with a bang. Two women entered and stopped at the bathroom mirror to talk. Some protective instinct convinced Maggie to wait inside the stall as the women chatted in front of the mirror.

So maybe she was still working out some of those *helpless ninny* issues, Maggie thought, shaking her head. Baby steps, after all.

"So, what happened?" the first one said, her voice low.

"Oh, my God, you won't believe it," the other one said, her inflection classic *Valley Girl*. She sounded about twelve years old. "One of their contest entries was tainted."

"That's terrible," the first woman said. "How?"

"Johnny said that someone broke into the storage room last night and tampered with the MacLaren entries. It wasn't discovered until this morning during the semifinal round of judging, about an hour ago. A couple of the judges tasted the MacLaren ale and a few minutes later, they lost their breakfasts. The head judge sampled it and declared it was ruined."

"But how'd anybody get into the storage room?"

Huddled behind the stall door, Maggie wanted to know the same thing. Who would do it? Why? And how?

And despite her lofty thoughts from a moment ago about facing confrontation, there was no way she was leaving her hiding place until she heard the whole story.

"I'm not sure," Valley Girl said. "They either found a key or just broke in. Johnny's mortified."

"Poor guy, it's not his fault," the first woman said. "Wow, so someone deliberately sabotaged the MacLarens. I wouldn't want to piss them off. Do they know who it is?"

"You have to ask?" Valley Girl said, her voice dripping sarcasm. "Who else could it be?"

There was a pause, and then the first woman whispered, "Oh, come on. You can't be serious."

"Connor is absolutely certain that she did it," Valley Girl said, her voice hushed but confident. "And look at the evidence. It happened during the dance last night. She arrived really late. And then later on, I saw her talking to Ted Blake. And it wasn't the first time, either. I've seen them together before. Connor saw them, too. They were very tight and cozy, if you know what I mean."

"Ted Blake?" the first woman whispered. "He hates the MacLarens. Do you think the two of them planned it together?"

Maggie's heart sank. She knew they were referring to her. And it was true that she'd talked to Ted Blake a few times, but she hadn't known what a rat he was until Connor told her. Her eyes narrowed in suspicion, almost certain she knew who "Valley Girl" was.

"Oh, absolutely," Valley Girl insisted, then fudged a bit. "Or she planned it alone. Either way, she's guilty as sin."

"But why would she do that to Connor?"

"She's jealous," Valley Girl hissed. "She'll do anything to win the competition, and that includes cheating."

"It doesn't make sense. Why would she sabotage Connor? She likes him."

"Because she can't have him back."

"News flash," the first woman said dryly. "She's sleeping in the same hotel room with him."

"That's only because he's paying her."

Maggie wondered if she had fallen down a rabbit hole. Their conversation sounded like a bad soap opera, and her head was starting to spin. And worst of all, she was sick to death of standing by idly while her reputation was being torn to shreds.

"He's paying her to sleep with him?"

"Yes, and I would've done it for free," Valley Girl whined.

"Lucinda, you're delusional," the first woman said. "You've had a crush on him since high school and he's never even looked at you. Face it, he's just not that into you."

"He would be if she would just go away."

Maggie's head was going to explode. She had to get out of here. It was time to take a risk, stop hiding, stop running from her mistakes. She had to fight for herself, for her reputation, for her life. And for Connor. Taking a deep breath, she gathered her strength and shoved the stall door open. "Hello, ladies."

Sarah saw her in the mirror and blinked in surprise.

Lucinda whirled around, then froze. Her face blanched and she stuttered in shock, "Wh-what are you…what… you…"

"Oh, shut up, Lucinda," Maggie said, dismissing her as she stepped up to the sink to wash her hands.

Sarah slowly shook her head. "Wow. I did not see that coming."

"Hello, Sarah," Maggie said pleasantly as she grabbed a towel from the dispenser.

Her old friend began to laugh. "Maggie, I was wondering how long it would take you to find your spine again."

Sarah was smiling in real pleasure and Maggie realized that maybe she hadn't lost all of her friends after all.

"Well, I've found it now, so look out." Maggie tossed the towel, then straightened her shoulders and shook her hair back defiantly as if she were about to go into battle. She looked at Sarah in the mirror. "You ain't seen nothin' yet."

"Go get 'em, Maggie," Sarah said, still laughing as Maggie stalked out of the bathroom.

Maggie stormed down the wide hallway to the judges' room entrance. She didn't much care what someone like Lucinda thought. What bothered her was that anyone else might think that she would resort to cheating. With a firm tug, she pulled the heavy door open. She no longer cared about contest rules and regulations. She had to find Connor and find out the truth. She wasn't about to take the word of a silly twit like Lucinda again.

The room was bustling. Dozens of judges sat at twenty

round tables scattered around the room. Each judge had at least five small glasses in front of them, each one marked with numbers only and filled with a different beer or ale. They were in various stages of tasting and studying and Maggie couldn't help being drawn into the process.

Each judge had a clipboard listing all of the categories used to judge the entries. Maggie knew them by heart. Appearance, aroma, flavor, balance, body and mouth feel, overall impression and flaws.

These judges took their job seriously, and the brewers who submitted their products to the competition were even more serious. Taking home these prizes could mean millions of dollars to the winner. The judges were trusted with making those critical decisions. And someone had destroyed that trust.

And they were blaming it on Maggie.

If Lucinda was to be believed, they'd already put her on trial and found her guilty.

But Lucinda was an idiot. Always had been. Would Connor actually take her word over Maggie's? It wasn't possible. She had to find Connor and hear the truth from him. After all this time they'd spent together, after all they'd shared, he had to realize that she would never do anything to hurt him. He had to know that she could be trusted with his heart.

She thought he already did. But now…was he still unsure of her feelings for him? Was he still holding on to the hurt he'd felt for so many years? They had talked about it over and over this week. How could he still believe she'd betrayed him back then?

She had to find him. But would he believe her? Would he trust her? Would he listen and believe it when she told him she'd never stopped loving him? That she loved him more than life itself?

She was confident that if she could just look into his

eyes, she would see the answers and know that he truly believed her, trusted her, loved her.

So where was he? The room was filled with people, but she could've picked him out of any crowd. And he was nowhere to be found.

"Where are you, Connor?" she murmured anxiously.

At that very moment, as if he'd been summoned by telepathic command, Connor walked out of a smaller anteroom and into the larger judges' room. He was followed by his brothers, the three of them looking like warriors marching into battle. All that was missing was the blue war paint and their clan tartans wrapped around them.

Johnny and two older men she didn't recognize followed in the brothers' wake. Their expressions were all severe and Maggie wouldn't want to tangle with any of them. But it appeared that they were headed in her general direction.

Connor's face was stern and ashen. Jake stared ahead with fierce intent, and Ian was fuming, as well.

Her heart went out to them. They looked angry and ready to fight. Maggie could completely understand their feelings, especially after overhearing Lucinda's unfounded accusations in the bathroom.

Then Connor spotted her. He led the men straight to her, watching her the entire time as he walked closer. Maggie stared back at him, searching for that same spark of love she'd seen in his eyes the night before. But all she saw was…guilt?

Blame?

Censure?

She couldn't tell, but she backed away instinctively as they got closer.

"Maggie, wait," Connor said.

She stopped and straightened her shoulders. "For what?" Sarah was right, she thought. Maggie had found her spine and she wouldn't be treated like a criminal. "For you and your brothers to pronounce me guilty? No, thank you." She turned to leave and slammed right into Lucinda, who was standing inches behind her.

"Don't believe her, Connor," Lucinda shouted.

"Lucinda," Jake said. "We were just looking for you."

Lucinda shot Maggie a look of triumph. "I was just looking for you guys, too."

"Connor," Maggie said. "I just heard about the tainted beer. I'm so sorry." But Connor wouldn't meet Maggie's gaze.

Why? Wait. He didn't believe her? Couldn't even look at her? Without even listening to her side of the story? So this was it?

Instead of meeting Maggie's gaze, he was staring at Lucinda.

"Your entries weren't damaged, Red," Johnny chimed in reassuringly.

"Thanks, Johnny," Maggie said, not reassured at all.

"So you only care about your own entries," Lucinda taunted. "Kind of selfish if you ask me."

"Nobody asked you," Maggie said.

"That's enough, Lucinda," Jake muttered.

"Me?" Lucinda slapped her hands on her hips in outrage. "She's the one pretending to be innocent. I'm just trying to point out who's guilty here."

Maggie looked carefully at each of the men in front of her and saw nothing encouraging in their eyes. "So you believe her? You think I'm…guilty?" She almost choked on the words. "You really believe I could do this?"

But Lucinda wasn't about to let them talk. Instead she confronted Maggie face-to-face. "What time did you finally show up at the dance?"

"What does that matter?" she asked.

Lucinda whipped around to the men. "She was late because she was busy sneaking into the storage room. You saw her talking to Ted Blake, Connor, I know you did. And that wasn't the only time I've seen them together. They probably planned it from the start."

Maggie frowned. The men were all watching Lucinda. Were they actually taking her word for this? Connor still wouldn't look at her and Maggie felt as if she were facing another inquisition, as she used to call her confrontations with her ex-husband and his mother.

Well, screw that. That was the past, she reminded herself. She would never, ever put up with an unfair accusation from anyone, ever again.

She gazed up at Connor. "Do you think I would do this to you?"

He stared hard at her, then said, "No."

"Wow," she whispered. "It took you more than a few seconds to decide on your answer. So your first instinct was to believe I would hurt you that way?"

His jaw tightened. "No, Maggie, it wasn't."

But again there was that momentary pause and Maggie began to question everything. Did he believe her? Did he trust her? Did he honestly think she would do this to him? If he believed she was innocent, then why wasn't he grabbing her and kissing her and assuring her that he knew she would never hurt him again?

Because he didn't believe that.

Her heart was breaking and she wanted to cry, to scream and demand that he believe her, love her, trust her.

But that would give Lucinda too much satisfaction. So instead Maggie cast one more beseeching glance at Connor, and when she received nothing back from him, not even a glance her way, she couldn't remain there another second. She turned and walked away.

"Maggie, wait," Connor said.

She wanted more than anything to keep moving away

from him, but she'd just remembered something important. She whipped around and walked up to Johnny.

"I'm signing my three Redhead entries over to the MacLaren Brewery," she said tersely. "I owe them the formulas anyway, so now they officially belong to Connor and his brothers. If you need me to sign anything swearing to that, text me. You have my phone number on my entry form."

She cast one more glance at Connor. "Oh, and you should fire your secretary."

And then she walked away.

He fired their secretary.

It was a unanimous decision made by all three brothers, especially after they viewed the videotape that had caught the culprit red-handed, so to speak.

Luckily for everyone, the convention center had videotapes running twenty-four hours a day, in every single room of the massive structure, including the storage room. Who knew? Connor thought, giving thanks that the center was so security-minded.

Connor, Jake and Ian had viewed the tape with Johnny and the festival president, along with the local sheriff, who had shown up for the festival on his day off. They had all seen the moment when their secretary Lucinda had snuck into the storage room and tainted one of the MacLaren entries.

But even before Connor saw the evidence, he had known Maggie was innocent, although Lucinda had done everything she could to sway their judgment in Maggie's direction.

But when Maggie stomped back over to Johnny and told him she was signing over her entries to MacLaren, Connor felt his heart jump in his chest. He could swear he'd never seen anything so courageous in his life. He'd been ready to tear off after her, but Lucinda was still raving and the sheriff needed their united presence.

"Don't tell me you believe her!" Lucinda had cried after Maggie stormed off. "Just because she put on a show for all of you, it doesn't mean anything. She's still your most viable suspect."

"What's your problem, Lucinda?" Connor asked, fed up with the woman sniping at Maggie. "What do you have against Maggie?"

"She's trying to hurt you. I'm trying to help you, but you can just forget it. I'm through doing all your dirty work." She spun around and began to walk away quickly.

"Not so fast, young lady," the sheriff said, jogging after her and grabbing hold of her arm. She squirmed and twisted to escape, but it was no use.

"Something you want to tell us, Lucinda?" Ian had said.

She stomped her foot. "I don't know why you think I did something. Maggie was the one who was talking to Ted Blake. Didn't you see her? The two of them were probably plotting the whole thing together. And look how late she was for the dance. She had plenty of time to break in and destroy the entry."

"It's not Maggie," Connor had said decisively, putting an end to Lucinda's blathering.

But he knew the damage had been done. Maggie had arrived right after he and his brothers had viewed the tapes. They all knew who the guilty party was. The videotape was a powerful indictment. But the sheriff had suggested it would be easier to deal with Lucinda if she would just confess. Connor had been willing to go along with his request, but regretted it the second he saw Maggie's reaction to his silence.

"Damn it." Connor should've grabbed her in his arms the instant Lucinda began to spew her venomous accusations. He'd been glaring at Lucinda, but she'd been standing directly behind Maggie. So now he wondered if Maggie might've thought his glares had been aimed at her.

"No doubt," Connor muttered, and rubbed his jaw in frustration. Maggie would naturally default to the worst-case scenario, and he couldn't really blame her in this situation.

She'd been through enough trauma in her life. Connor was sick at the thought that he might've given her a reason to doubt that he was completely, utterly, irrevocably in love with her.

Now he needed to find her and convince her otherwise.

Maggie barely made it to the suite and got the door closed before the tears threatened to fall.

But she was sick to death of tears. Yes, her heart was breaking, but she refused to cry about it.

And to think that she'd gone downstairs to find Connor and tell him she'd fallen in love with him. She had foolishly thought he'd be happy to hear it and would respond by telling her how much he loved her, too.

How ironic. It seemed that circumstances had played a cruel joke on her. It wouldn't be the first time.

So much for taking risks.

"Now you're just feeling sorry for yourself," she muttered. "But don't you dare cry." She grabbed her suitcase and opened it on the bed. Then she began to toss her clothes into the open bag.

She couldn't wait to leave this damn hotel and go home to Grandpa and the goats.

"Goats? Really?" She sniffled a little at the thought of the goats, then rolled her eyes. How pathetic could she get? She was reduced to depending on goats to comfort and sympathize with her in her moment of misery. It just added to the misery.

She heard the suite door open and knew that Connor

had come back. Could things get any worse? She wanted to hide under the bed, but she'd been hiding for way too long. No more hiding, Maggie. She'd grown so much in the past few years, and these past few days had made her feel more powerful than she ever had.

Besides, it was a platform bed, so there was no place to hide anyway.

She really didn't want another confrontation with Connor, but she couldn't avoid it now and she figured it was long past due. But at least she knew that his last impression of her would not be of red-rimmed, swollen eyes and tear-drenched cheeks. Nope. She was not going to cry and look like some pathetic water rat.

But then, why would he care what she looked like? He thought she was a saboteur—or worse.

He stood in the doorway, watching her.

"Hello, Connor," she said, and dropped her shoes into the suitcase. "Did something else happen that you can accuse me of doing? Maybe I tainted the water supply? Released a dirty bomb? Stole your underwear? Take your best shot."

"I'm not here to accuse you of anything, Maggie."

"Good," she said, folding her arms across her chest defensively. "Because I'm not putting up with one more accusation from you or anyone else. If you honestly believe that I would ever do anything like that to hurt you, you're horribly mistaken." She grabbed another shirt from the closet and flung it into the suitcase. "My God, what you must think of me. One of those judges could've been killed. Do you really think I'm capable of that?"

"No."

"Right." She tossed a pair of pants into the suitcase. "Look, this has been fun. Well, most of it, anyway. The past hour or so, not so much. But other than that whole belittling, accusing thing that just happened downstairs, I had a really wonderful time and I'll always keep the memory of you in my heart."

And with those words said, she burst into tears. Damn it. She really didn't want to cry. She was stronger now. But the truth was bringing her to her knees. Connor had always been in her heart and he would remain there forever, even if they were apart.

Still, tears were not acceptable. She hastily brushed them away as she grabbed more clothes and threw them into the suitcase.

"I'm glad to hear it," he said, "because you'll always be in my heart, too."

"Thank you." She sniffled.

"And I owe you this," he said, handing her a piece of paper.

Her eyes were still a little blurry, but she could see it was a check with a lot of numbers written on it. He was paying her for her week of service. Another sob escaped and she had to struggle to speak. "Do you really think I'm going to take this?"

"That was the deal," he said.

She took a deep breath and wiped her eyes. Then she gazed at him for a long moment. "Forget the deal," she said finally, and tore the check in two.

"Maggie," he said softly.

"Connor, I saw that look of accusation in your eyes."

"That look you saw," he said with aggravating calmness, "was aimed at Lucinda, who was standing about two feet behind you the whole time."

"If you say so," she muttered.

"You know she was there, right?" Connor took one step into the room. "She was the one we were all looking at. We already knew she was guilty. We reviewed the videotapes a few minutes before you arrived. We saw her do it, Maggie."

"Videotapes?"

"Yeah. The center runs security videos in all the rooms," he explained. "So we knew Lucinda was guilty. But even before I saw the tape, it never crossed my mind to suspect you, Maggie. Why would I? You're in love with me. You would never hurt me."

She glared at him. "How do you know?"

He laughed, damn him. He wasn't playing fair. She'd wanted to be the one to tell him she loved him, had rushed downstairs to find him and let him know her feelings. But he'd guessed anyway before she could say the words. But wait, she thought. He hadn't said he loved her, too. Why? She knew he loved her. Or he *did,* before this day happened.

"You got caught in the cross fire," he continued. "The sheriff wanted her to confess, so he advised us not to say anything. But he finally got tired of her caterwauling and dragged her off to book her."

That got her attention. "Really? You had her arrested?"

"Hell, yes," he said, scowling. "You were right, Maggie. She could've killed one of those judges."

Her anger left her in a heartbeat and she had to lean against the dresser to steady her suddenly weak knees.

"So let me turn the question around on you," Connor said softly, taking another step farther into the room and disturbing what little equilibrium she had left.

"What question?" she asked warily.

He took a step closer. "Do you really think I'm capable of believing you could do such a horrible thing?"

"Oh." She stared at him in shock, then had to think about what he'd said. "No. Of course not, but we've had to overcome some history to—"

"I'd say we've overcome all that." Another step. "So now, do you really think I believe you could hurt me that way?"

She bit her lip. "When you put it like that, no. But I still think—"

"Don't think." He was inches away now, close enough to

reach out and tenderly sweep a strand of hair off her face. His fingers remained, lightly stroking her cheek. "Don't think, Maggie. Feel. Take a chance. Believe. In me. In us. I do."

"I do, too," she whispered. "I believe in us. I believe in taking a chance. Risking it all. For you."

He kissed the edge of her chin. "I'm so in love with you, Maggie."

"Oh." She had to catch her breath. "I—I love you so much, Connor. I don't think I've ever stopped loving you."

"I've never stopped loving you, either."

"I'm so sorry I wasted so much time being away from you."

"Let's make up for it now," he said. "Say you'll marry me, Maggie?"

"Oh, Connor," she said, staring up at him. Her heart filled with so much joy she wasn't sure she could hold it all. "Yes, of course I'll marry you."

"And love me always?" He kissed her cheek.

"You know I will," she whispered.

He nibbled her neck. "And have my children?"

"Oh, Connor." She blinked away more tears. "Yes. I would love to have children with you."

He licked her earlobe. "And pick out my clothes for me?"

She laughed and smacked his chest, then threw her arms around his neck. "Yes. Absolutely yes to all of the above."

"I'm glad you're packing your bags," he said, glancing around the room. "Let's go home right now and start our lives together."

"Please, Connor," she said as he swept her off her feet and into his arms. "Take me home."

Epilogue

"I heard from the Scottish lawyers again," Jake said, leaning back in his chair as he downed his beer. "They're getting more nervous about the property, so I told them that one of us would fly over to check things out."

Connor's brothers had come by his house to talk business and to try a taste of Maggie's latest award-winning ale. Connor had named it Maggie's Pride, a takeoff of their own MacLaren's Pride. "Ian's the logical choice to go."

Ian scowled. "Just because my ex-father-in-law lives there doesn't mean I'm the one who has to go. Forget it."

"Why not?" Jake asked.

Ian glared at him but said nothing. He'd been doing that a lot lately, Connor realized. Something had crawled up his butt, but he wasn't willing to talk about it. It wasn't too hard to figure out, though, since he and his wife, Samantha, were no longer living together.

"Well, don't look at me," Connor said. "I'm not leaving Maggie."

At that moment, Connor's beautiful wife walked into the room carrying two bowls of chips and salsa and set them on the table in front of the men. Her gaze went directly to Connor. "You're leaving me?"

Jake laughed. "No, he's not leaving you. He just married you. I haven't seen him wander more than five feet away from you since the wedding."

"Come here," Connor said, smiling up at Maggie. He grabbed her hand and pulled her gently onto his lap. Then he wrapped his arms around her waist and felt utterly content with life.

He hadn't announced the news to his brothers yet, but Maggie had been to the doctor yesterday, where they found out that she was pregnant. Connor wasn't sure he could contain all the love he had inside for his wife and the tiny baby growing within her belly.

It had barely been a month after the festival ended when he and Maggie were married on the beach with their family and a few trusted friends gathered around to celebrate. They had been apart for so many years that neither of them had wanted to wait any longer to begin their married life together. The small ceremony had suited Maggie perfectly. She'd already endured an extravagant society wedding with her ex-husband and didn't want to repeat the experience.

And speaking of her bizarre ex-husband, Connor had not been surprised to hear the news that Ashford had recently been arrested on suspicion of murdering his dear mother. According to the news reports Connor had seen, it appeared that the old woman hadn't died of natural causes after all. Her cantankerous butler had hounded the police until they agreed to investigate and finally discovered the truth.

Maggie snuggled closer and Connor kissed her neck, thankful again that she had come back home to him. The day she told him she was ready to take the biggest risk of her life and marry him, he knew he was the luckiest man alive.

"Jeez, you two," Ian groused. "Get a room."

Connor laughed, unfazed by his brother's bad mood. "Ignore him, he's jealous."

"He's especially cranky today," Jake said.

"Stop talking about me like I'm not in the room," Ian protested. "Besides, you would be cranky, too, if…never mind."

"If what?" Connor asked, growing concerned. He'd

never seen his brother more miserable. Ian had always been the most even-tempered of the three brothers, but ever since he'd separated from his wife, Samantha, he'd been unhappy.

Ian shoved his hand through his dark hair in frustration. "Never mind."

"Now you've got our curiosity piqued," Jake said mildly.

"You'll get over it," Ian muttered.

"I still don't see why you can't go to Scotland," Connor said, looking at Ian pointedly. "You loved it there last time. And Gordon is a great host."

"Yeah, well, last time I went, I was with Gordon's daughter," Ian reminded them. "Things have changed."

"No kidding," Jake said, took a last gulp of beer and set his glass on the table.

Maggie turned and gave Connor a look of concern, then glanced at his brother. "I'm sorry, Ian. Connor would go, but the timing—"

"No, love," Connor interrupted, not yet willing to share their baby news. He gave her a quick hug. "They understand that I won't be going this time."

Jake stood and stretched. "Fine, I'll go. I should've just agreed to go in the first place. Better than listening to Ian whine."

"I don't whine," Ian whined.

Maggie giggled.

"It's better if you go, anyway, Jake," Connor said. "You'll do the job quickly and get home."

"Yeah, I'll make it a fast trip, but I still want to stop in Kilmarnock for a day and visit Gordon. If Ian's really going to divorce Samantha, it's more important than ever to maintain a strong contact with her father."

"No," Ian said, more forcefully than usual.

"What do you mean, no?" Connor said. "Are you getting a divorce or not?"

Restless, Ian pushed his chair back from the table and stood. "I mean, no. You can't stop to see Gordon."

Jake whipped around. "Why the hell not?"

"Because he's disappeared," Ian said. "Nobody's seen him for days and they don't have a clue where he's gone." And with that bombshell dropped, he left the room abruptly.

Jake and Connor exchanged looks of apprehension. Then Jake shrugged. "You know Gordon. Chances are he slipped away to be with a woman. Let's not jump to conclusions."

"That's the most likely answer," Connor said, nodding in agreement. Right now he had to admit he was more concerned about his brother than Gordon McGregor's whereabouts. He wasn't sure what was going on with Ian and his in-laws, but it was something Connor would have to deal with later on. Much later, he thought, after he'd had more time to spend with his beautiful new wife and the unborn child they had created.

Maggie reach for his hand and whispered, "I love you."

"I know," Connor said, making her smile as he leaned over and kissed her with all his heart.

* * * * *

If you liked this story, try these other novels from New York Times *bestselling author Kate Carlisle:*

THE MILLIONAIRE MEETS HIS MATCH
SWEET SURRENDER, BABY SURPRISE
HOW TO SEDUCE A BILLIONAIRE
AN INNOCENT IN PARADISE
SHE'S HAVING THE BOSS'S BABY

All available now, from Harlequin Desire!

COMING NEXT MONTH FROM

H HARLEQUIN®

Desire

Available January 7, 2014

#2275 FOR THE SAKE OF THEIR SON
The Alpha Brotherhood • Catherine Mann
They'd been the best of friends, but after one night of passion everything changed. A year later, Lucy Ann and Elliot have a baby, but is their child enough to make them a family?

#2276 BENEATH THE STETSON
Texas Cattleman's Club: The Missing Mogul
Janice Maynard
Rancher Gil Addison has few opportunities for romance, but he may have found a woman who can love him *and* his son. If only she wasn't investigating him and his club!

#2277 THE NANNY'S SECRET
Billionaires and Babies • Elizabeth Lane
Wyatt needs help when his teenager brings home a baby, but he never expects to fall for the nanny. Leigh seems almost too good to be true—until her startling revelation changes everything.

#2278 PREGNANT BY MORNING
Kat Cantrell
One magical night in Venice brings lost souls Matthew and Evangeline together. With their passionate affair inching dangerously toward something more, one positive pregnancy test threatens to drive them apart for good.

#2279 AT ODDS WITH THE HEIRESS
Las Vegas Nights • Cat Schield
Hotelier Scarlett may have inherited some dangerous secrets, but the true risk is to her heart when the man she loves to hate, security entrepreneur Logan, decides to make her safety his business.

#2280 PROJECT: RUNAWAY BRIDE
Project: Passion • Heidi Betts
Juliet can't say *I do*, so she runs out on her own wedding. But she can't hide for long when Reid, private investigator—and father of her unborn child—is on the case.

YOU CAN FIND MORE INFORMATION ON UPCOMING HARLEQUIN® TITLES, FREE EXCERPTS AND MORE AT WWW.HARLEQUIN.COM.

HDCNM1213